★ Tormyle was a nine-foot ogre who could not be slain.

★ *Tormyle was a knight on horseback —with no face behind the helmet.*

★ Tormyle was a scaly fire-breathing dragon.

★ *Tormyle was a lovely songstress who could enchant every heart.*

★ Tormyle was all of these and none of these—because Tormyle was really a sunless world wandering lifeless between the galaxies.

★ *For Earl Dumarest and the real Mayenne, Tormyle was a rescuer and an inquisitor. To escape from that world was impossible without the assistance of Tormyle. And Tormyle would let none go who could not answer the unanswerable.*

MAYENNE

by
E. C. TUBB

DAW BOOKS, INC.
DONALD A. WOLLHEIM, PUBLISHER

1301 Avenue of the Americas
New York, N. Y.   10019

To

Hilda Elizabeth Mitchell

FIRST PRINTING, MAY 1973

2 3 4 5 6 7 8 9

PRINTED IN U.S.A.

Chapter

◆ **ONE** ◆

Dumarest heard the sound as he left his cabin, a thin, penetrating wail, almost a scream, then he relaxed as he remembered the Ghenka who had joined the ship at Frell. She was in the salon, entertaining the company with her undulating song, accompanying herself with the crystalline tintinnabulation of tiny bells. She wore the full Ghenka costume, her body covered, her face a mask of paint, the curlicues of gold and silver, ruby and jet set with artfully placed gems which caught and reflected the light in splinters of darting brilliance so that her features seemed to be alive with jeweled and crawling insects.

She was, he assumed, no longer young. No Ghenka in her prime would be found on a vessel plying this far from the center of the galaxy; rich worlds and wealthy patrons were too far apart. Someone on the decline, he guessed, unable or unwilling to meet rising competition, going to where she would be both novel and entrancing. Not that it mattered. Whatever her age there was no denying the trained magic of her voice.

He leaned back against the wall and allowed the hypnotic cadences to wash over his conscious mind, dulling reality and triggering sequences of unrelated imagery. A wide ocean beneath an emerald sky. A slender girl seated on a rock, her hair a ripple of purest silver as it streamed in the wind, the lines of her body the epitome of grace. A fire and a ring of intent faces, leaping flames and the distant keening of mourning women. Ice glittering as it fell in splintered shards, ringing in crystal destruction. Goblets shattering and spilling blood-red wine, the chime of chandeliers, the hiss of meeting blades, harsh, feral, the turgid chill of riding Low.

"Fascinating." The low voice at his side broke his reverie. Chom Roma held unsuspected depths of artistic appreciation. The plump hand he raised to stroke his jowl, matted with hair and gaudy with rings, trembled a little. "Fascinating," he repeated. "And dangerous. Such a song can lead a man into memories he would prefer to forget. For a moment there I was young again, a slim boy flushed with the triumph of his first sale. And there was a girl with lambent eyes and skin the hue of a pearl." He fell silent, brooding, then shook his head. "No, Earl, such dreams are not for men like us."

Dumarest made no comment; softly as the entrepreneur had spoken his voice had been a jarring irritation. There would be time for talk later, but now the spell was too strong and, he agreed, too dangerous. A man should not become enamored of mental imagery. The past was dead, to resurrect it, even by song-induced stimulation, was unwise.

Ignoring the Ghenka he concentrated instead on the salon and the company it contained. Both were familiar from countless repetitions; a low room fitted with tables and chairs, dispensers against a wall, the floor scarred with usage and time. The assembly a collection of men and women with money enough to afford a High passage, their metabolism slowed by the magic of quick-time so that an hour became a minute, months shortened into days. Yet even so the journey was tedious; in this part of the galaxy worlds were none too close, and entertainment, because of that, the more highly appreciated.

The song ended and he heard a ragged sigh as the bells fell silent, the company blinking a little, silent as they regretted lost imagery, then breaking the tension with a storm of applause. A shower of coins fell at the Ghenka's feet and she stooped, gathering them up, bowing as she left the salon. Dumarest caught her eyes as she passed close to where he stood, deep pits of smoldering jet flecked with scarlet. Her perfume was sharp, almost acrid, and yet not unpleasant.

Quietly he said, "Thank you, my lady, for the display of

your skill. A truly remarkable performance. The company is honored."

"You are most gracious, my lord." Even when speaking her voice held a wailing lilt. "I have other songs if you would care to hear them. If you would prefer a private session it could be arranged."

"I will consider it." Dumarest added more coins to the heap clutched in her hand. "In the meantime again receive my thanks."

It was dismissal, but she did not leave. "You go to Selegal, my lord?"

"Yes."

"I also. It may be that we shall meet again. If so it would be my pleasure."

"And mine," said Dumarest.

Still she lingered. "You will pardon me if I cause offense, my lord, but, as you probably know, I travel alone. To one in my profession such a thing is not wise. Also, on Selegal, I will be unfamiliar with the local ways. I am not suited to the arrangement of business ventures. Perhaps, if you would consider it, something could be arranged."

Dumarest caught the note of appeal, the desperate need that broke through the stilted formality which was a part of her professional training. A woman alone, most likely afraid, doing her best to survive in a region foreign to her experience. Yet he had no intention of getting involved.

Before he could refuse she said, "You will consider it, my lord? At least your advice would be of value. Perhaps we could meet later—in my cabin?"

"Perhaps," said Dumarest.

Chom Roma drew in his breath as the woman moved on to her quarters. "A conquest, Earl. The woman finds you pleasing and a man could do worse than take her under his protection. Had she made me such an offer I would not have hesitated." Envy thickened his voice a little. "But then I am not tall and strong and with a face that commands respect. I am only old Chom who buys and sells and makes a profit where he can. A stranger to courts and the places where the rich and high-born gather. A woman can tell these things."

"Some women do not regard that as important."

"True, but the Ghenka is not one of them." Chom

glanced down the corridor to the closing door of her
cabin. "She lives for her art and herself like all her kind.
Could you imagine such a woman living in a hut? Tilling
fields or working in a factory? She needs someone to stand
between her and the harshness of life. A strong protector
and someone to take care of unpleasant details. I wonder
what happened to her manager. Perhaps he tried to sell
her and she had other ideas. A knife in the dark, a drop
of poison, who can tell? These things happen." He
shrugged, thick shoulders heaving beneath the ornamented
fabric of his blouse. "Well, Earl, such is life. What now?
Shall we try our luck?"

Dumarest glanced to where the gambler sat at his table
ringed by a handful of players. Harg Branst was a thin
man with prominent ears, his features vulpine and touched
by advancing years. A true professional, he wore no rings
and his nails were neatly trimmed. He rode on a profit-
sharing basis, as much a part of the ship's furnishings as
the steward and cabins. He looked up from his cards, met
Dumarest's eyes, and made a slight gesture of invitation
for him to join the game.

Chom spoke in a whisper. "Have you noticed his good
fortune? Never does he seem to lose. Now, to me, that is
against all the laws of chance."

"So?"

"Perhaps something could be arranged between us? I
have a little skill, and you are no stranger to the gaming
table. It would be a kindness to teach him a lesson."

Dumarest said, dryly, "At a profit, naturally."

"All men must pay to learn," said Chom blandly. "Some
do it with their lives. We need not be so harsh. It will be
enough, I think, to trim his wings a little. Working together it could easily be done—a matter of distraction at
a critical moment. You understand?"

The palming of cards, the switch, the squeeze when,
convinced that he could not lose, the gambler would allow
greed to dull his caution. It could be done, granted the
basic skill, but unless the man was a fool the odds were
against it. And no man who earned his living at the tables
could be that much of a fool.

"The cost of the journey," urged Chom. "A High passage safe in our pockets when we land. Insurance in case

of need. You agree?" He scowled at the lack of response. "A golden opportunity, Earl. Almost a gift. I cannot understand why you refuse. We—" He broke off as if knowing it was useless to argue. "Well, what else to kill the time? Daroca has some wine. Come, let us test his generosity."

Dumarest frowned, the man was beginning to annoy him. A shipboard acquaintance, met when he had joined the ship at Zelleth, the entrepreneur was becoming a nuisance. Deliberately he looked away, studying the others in the salon. Two dour men, brothers, Sac and Tek Qualish, consultant engineers now intent on their cards. Mari Analoch, hard, old, with eyes like those of a bird of prey, a procuress seeking to open a new establishment. A squat amazon, Hera Phollen with her charge the Lady Lolis Egas, young, spoiled, eager for excitement and adulation. Vekta Gorlyk, who played like a machine. Ilgazt Bitola, who played like a fool. The man who waited with his wine.

"Earl?" Chom was insistent.

"No."

"You have something better to do? More study, perhaps?" Chom smiled as Dumarest turned to stare into his eyes. "The steward was careless and failed to close the door of your cabin. I saw the papers you had been working on. Such dedication! But I am not after charity, Earl. Daroca wants to meet you and I think it would profit you to meet him." He paused and added, softly: "It is possible that he might be able to tell you something of Earth."

Eisach Daroca was a slight man, tall, dressed in somber fabrics of expensive weave, the starkness relieved only by the jeweled chain hanging around his neck, the wide bracelets on his wrists. He wore a single ring on the third finger of his left hand, a seal intricately engraved and mounted on a thick band. His face was smooth, soft, the skin like crepe around the eyes. His hair was clubbed and thickly touched with silver. A dilettante, Dumarest had decided. A man with wealth enough to follow his whims, perhaps jaded, perhaps a genuine seeker after knowledge. An eternal student. Such men were to be found in unexpected places.

He rose as they approached, smiling, extending his hand. "My dear Chom, I'm so glad that you managed to persuade your friend to join us. You will join me in wine, Earl? I may call you that? Please be seated."

The wine was an emerald perfume, delicate to the nose, tart and refreshing to the tongue. Daroca served it in goblets of iron-glass, thin as a membrane, decorated with abstract designs, expensive and virtually indestructible. A part of his baggage, Dumarest knew, as was the wine, the choice foods he ate. Not for him the usual basic, the spigot-served fluid laced with vitamins, sharp with citrus, sickly with glucose, which formed the normal diet of those traveling High. Everything about the man spoke of wealth and culture, but what was he doing on a vessel like this? Bluntly he asked the question.

"A man must travel as he can," said Daroca. "And it amuses me to venture down the byways of space. To visit the lesser worlds untouched by the larger ships. And yet I do not believe there is virtue to be gained by suffering hardship. There is no intrinsic merit in pain and, surely, discomfort is a minor agony to be avoided whenever possible. You agree?"

"At least it is an interesting philosophy."

"I like my comforts," said Chom. He lowered his empty glass. "The trouble is in being able to afford them. More often than not it isn't easy."

Daroca refilled his glass. "And you, Earl? Do you also enjoy comfort?"

"He's had too much of the rough not to enjoy the smooth," said Chom before Dumarest could answer. "I can tell these things. There is a look about a man who has lived hard, a set of the lips, the jaw, an expression in the eyes. The way he walks and stands, little things, but betraying. As there is with a woman," he continued, musingly. "You can tell the one who is willing and the one who is not. The one who is seeking and the one who has found." He took a mouthful of wine. "What did you think of the Ghenka?"

"She has skill." Daroca glanced at Dumarest. "More wine?"

"Later, perhaps."

"Is the vintage not to your liking?"

"It is too good to be hurried."

"As is interesting conversation. I contend that intelligent discourse is the hallmark of civilized man. As yet I have found no evidence to shake my conviction, but plenty to uphold it. You are satisfied with the wine, Chom?"

The plump man dabbed at his lips, his second glass almost empty. If he caught the irony he gave no sign of it. Instead he said, "She is more than skilled. The Ghenka, I mean. She is a true artist. Did you know that it takes twenty years to train such a one? The voice has to reach full maturity and they begin learning as soon as they can talk. Twenty years," he brooded. "A lifetime. But with such a woman what more could a man want?"

"A place of his own, perhaps," said Daroca softly. "A home. Children to bear his name and continue his line. Some men are not so easily satisfied, as I am sure Earl would agree. The mood of a moment does not last. It holds within itself the seeds of its own destruction. Passion is a flame which devours what it feeds on. The satisfaction of conquest, of possession, fades to be replaced by new aims. The happy man is the one who finds contentment with what he has."

Dumarest made no comment, sitting back in his chair, watching, savoring the wine. He was curious as to why Daroca should have wanted his company. Boredom, perhaps, but that was too facile an answer. The salon held others to whom he could have given his wine. An audience, then, someone to listen while he spoke? But why the crude and grossly coarse entrepreneur? Why himself?

Caution pricked its warning and yet the man seemed harmless enough, even though it was obvious he had arranged the meeting. And even if he weren't harmless there might be information to be gained. It was barely possible that he knew something of Earth and, if he did, the time would be well spent.

Dumarest looked down at his hand. The knuckles were white from the pressure with which he gripped the goblet. Deliberately he relaxed. Haste now would gain nothing, and hope was not to be encouraged. Also, Chom could have lied.

Quietly he said, "I understand that you have traveled much and far. May I ask why?"

"Why I travel?" Daroca shrugged, a gesture of pure elegance when compared to Chom's heaving shoulders. "As I told you, it amuses me to visit other worlds, to study other cultures. The galaxy is incredibly vast when considered in terms of habitable planets, and there are intriguing backwaters, lost worlds, almost, rarely visited and of an engrossing nature to one like myself who is a student of mankind. May I return the question? You also travel. Your reason?"

"I have a restless nature," said Dumarest. "And I like variety."

"A kindred spirit," said Daroca. "Shall we drink to our mutual interest?"

He was casual as he lifted his goblet, but his eyes were shrewd. A dilettante, perhaps, but Dumarest recognized that he was no fool. Only such would have taken him for a man of cultured leisure, even if Chom had not spoken as he had. Travel took money and a High passage was not cheap. Those who couldn't afford it rode Low, sealed in the caskets usually reserved for livestock, doped, frozen, ninety percent dead, gambling their lives against the fifteen percent death rate for the privilege of traveling cheap.

To such travel was a mania or a grim necessity.

"He's looking for something," said Chom as Daroca lowered his glass. "A planet named Earth."

"Earth?"

"That's right." The entrepreneur reached, uninvited, for the wine. "A crazy name for a world. You might as well call it dirt, or ground, or soil. Earth!" He drank greedily, and dabbed at his lips. "A dream. How can there be such a place? It doesn't make sense."

"A mythical planet?" Daroca shrugged. "There are many such. Worlds of supposed fantastic wealth, once found and then, for some reason, lost or forgotten. Once I went in quest of such a place. Need I say that it was a futile search?"

"It has another name," said Dumarest softly. "Terra. Perhaps you have heard of it?"

For a moment time seemed to congeal, to halt as he waited, his outward calm belying his inner tension. Perhaps, this time, he would receive a positive answer. Perhaps this wanderer would know the way to the planet he sought. Then, as Daroca slowly shook his head, the moment passed.

"You have never heard of it?"

"I am sorry, my friend, but I have never been to the world you mention."

"It doesn't exist, that's why." Chom was emphatic. "Why do we sit here talking about such things? There is wine to be drunk and beauty to admire. A pity we could not combine the two. Come, Earl, stop looking so bleak. At least you have the consolation of wine and there is always the Ghenka. A pleasant combination, yes?"

"For some," admitted Daroca. "For others, perhaps not. Such men are not so easily pleased. But I offer a toast. To success in all we attempt." He paused and added softly: "To Earth!"

"To a dream," scoffed Chom. He emptied his glass in a single gulp.

Chapter

◆ TWO ◆

The Lady Lolis Egas was bored. She lifted an arm and watched as the sheer fabric of her gown slid, slowly at first, then with an acceleration so fast it was impossible to follow, down the smooth length of her arm. It was a trick induced by the drug in her blood; the use of quick-time held peculiar dangers and played visual distortions. The sleeve had moved at a normal rate, only to her and those with her had it seemed to travel so fast.

As the cards which left the dealer's hands, the container which one of the players knocked from its place, the coins which the old harridan insisted on throwing instead of, as was normal, sliding them across the surface of the table.

The lifted arm, now bare to the shoulder, was flawless. She turned it, allowing the light to catch the gems on wrist and fingers, the great sapphire of her betrothal ring shimmering with ice-cold fire. It was a good ring and there would be more like it, clothes too, rare perfumes, expensive foods. Alora Motril of the House of Ayette would make a good husband.

But the nuptials were yet to come and, now, she was bored.

"Perhaps you should rest, my lady." Hera Phollen recognized the signs, and made the suggestion more from hope than any conviction that she would be obeyed. Her charge would be no trouble once asleep. "We have far to go and you will want to look your best when we arrive."

"Am I so ugly?"

"You are beautiful, my lady."

Hera's voice was deep, her hair short and her face seamed, but she was not a man and Lolis had little desire

14

for the adulation of women. She lowered her arm and turned, studying those in the salon. Vekta Gorlyk? Perhaps, but there was something cold about him, something remote; he would offer little sport. Polite, yes, and with time it would be possible to arouse his passion, but he lacked the ability of quick interplay, and while it would be amusing to shatter his reserve, it would take a patience she didn't possess. Ilgazt Bitola? He was young with a foppish manner of dress and his face held a certain weakness which she had long since learned to recognize. He would be willing to amuse her and yet the conquest would be too easy. Who then?

Her eyes drifted toward the table at which the three men sat. She dismissed Daroca at once, he was too world-wise, too cynical and, perhaps, too cautious to respond to her bait. The entrepreneur was too gross. Dumarest?

Softly she said, "Tell me, Hera, could you defeat that man?"

"In combat, my lady?"

"Naturally, what else?"

"Perhaps, my lady. It is something I would prefer not to put to the test."

"Afraid, Hera?"

The gibe was too obvious and the girl too transparent to arouse anger. Quietly she said, "My lady, I am to deliver you safe and unsullied to your husband to be. If it becomes necessary I will kill to achieve that aim. And there is no man alive of whom I am afraid."

Lolis could believe it. The amazon was trained and incredibly strong, a fitting guard for such as herself. A man she could have seduced, but not Hera, and the woman was dedicated to her profession. Yet it was amusing to tease her.

She rose and stretched, accentuating the curves of her body. At the gaming table Ilgazt Bitola watched and called an invitation.

"Are you going to join us, my lady?"

"Gambling bores me," she said. "And I am already bored."

"So?" He was eager to please. "Perhaps that could be

cured? An examination of the vessel, for example. Just you and I. Alone."

"I have already seen the ship."

"But not all of it, my lady," he insisted. "There is an unusual beast in the hold and one well worth your attention. I am sure the handler will not object." He let a stream of coins fall ringingly from his hand. "I have the means to persuade him if you agree."

She shrugged and turned away so as to face the three men sitting over their wine. Smiling, she approached them. Daroca courteously rose.

"My lady?"

"May I join you?"

"Certainly. A moment and I will summon the steward to bring more glasses."

"That will not be necessary." She stooped over the table, ignoring Chom's lascivious eyes, the inhaled breath of Hera's disapproval, and lifted Dumarest's goblet. She drank and replaced it, the mark of her lips clear against the crystal. "Thank you."

It was a simple approach, and, from experience, predictable. He would now lift the glass and drink and make some remark as to how sweet her lips had made the wine. Casual banter without real meaning, but which could lead to other things. She would sit beside him and they would talk, and, later perhaps, she would no longer be bored.

The prospect excited her, his masculinity triggering her overdeveloped sexual characteristics so that she felt the biological reaction begin to take command. Watching, Hera felt a quick disgust. Couldn't the stupid young fool recognize the difference between men? Did she think that Dumarest would react as, say, the entrepreneur would in similar circumstances? Across the girl's shoulder she met his eyes, and relaxed as she saw the quiet amusement. There was no danger here.

Chom said, "Sit, my lady. Your presence sweetens the wine and, should you care to drink from my glass, my happiness would be complete."

She looked at Dumarest. "And yours?"

"Happiness is not such a simple thing nor is it so easily obtained. If you would care to finish the wine, my lady?"

He rose and offered her his chair. "I have drunk enough. You will excuse me?"

It was rejection and she felt a surge of anger so intense as to make her feel physically ill. Hera's smile made things no better, but the time for revenge was not yet. Later she would think of a way, but, for now, it was important to salvage her pride.

"I had no intention of staying," she said coldly. "You presume to think otherwise. I will see you later, Daroca, when you have more congenial company. In the meantime I have other things to do." To Bitola she called, "You were going to show me something in the hold. How long must I wait?"

Harg Branst riffled the cards, cut and dealt sliding each across the table. He said, "You have made an enemy, Earl. If I were you I should be careful. That guard of hers is an ugly customer."

Mari Analoch scowled at her hand, rings flashing on her wrinkled fingers. "She's a stupid, oversexed bitch, and that kind are always trouble. I should know. In my business they are more bother than worth. The men like them, sure, but they love to set one against the other and they can change at the drop of a coin. Do you call these cards?"

"I'll change hands if you want," said Chom. "They can't be worse than mine."

The dour brothers said nothing, playing with a grim determination. Vekta Gorlyk carefully stacked his hand. Dumarest watched the neat precision of his movements, the immobility of his face, the eyes which alone seemed alive. Odd eyes, veiled, secretive.

Daroca moved coins to the center of the table. "I'll bet five."

"Earl?"

"And five more."

"She's going to Ayette," said Mari. "Getting married, so I hear. The poor fool doesn't know what he's letting himself in for. He'll pay for every ounce of pleasure he gets and he'll be wearing horns before a month is past. I'd bet on it."

"Bet on your hand," suggested Harg. "And you're

wrong. She's marrying high and there'll be enough guards around to keep her pure. Even so, Earl, I wouldn't visit that world if I were you. Chom?"

"I'll stay."

"Mari?"

"This hand is like the girl, pretty to look at but useless for anything else." She threw the cards aside. "With your luck, Harg, we should be partners. How about that? I've a nice little place lined up on Selegal, and if you've got some cash you could do a lot worse. With me running the girls and you the tables we should do well. Interested?"

"I might be," said Harg. He leaned back, knowing there was no need for high concentration, that the game had lost its sharp edge and that the players were sitting more for social reasons than anything else. And the prospect was attractive. He was getting tired of the limited life of endless journeyings broken only by brief halts at various planets. And, always, was the possibility that his luck might run out, his skill become blunted. The woman offered security. "I might be interested," he said again. "Let me think about it."

"How about you, Earl?" Mari was shrewd, her eyes calculating as she glanced at where he sat. "My experience, Harg's luck and you to give protection. We split the profits three ways and it won't cost you much to buy in. In my business you need a strong man around to keep order and take care of the parasites."

"Try the amazon," suggested Earl. "She might be interested."

"And you're not?"

"No."

"He spends his life throwing away opportunities," said Chom. "The Ghenka, the girl and now you. Some men have too much luck." He frowned at his cards. "I'll take two."

"Wait your turn," said Harg. "Earl raised and now it's up to Daroca."

"Take it easy," Chom pleaded as Daroca fingered his coins. "Think of the poor."

Mari snorted. "Let the monks do that. That's one good thing about this journey. No monks. I was on a ship once carrying two of them. The Universal Brotherhood might

do a lot of good work, but there are times when they
don't belong. You know, they made me feel guilty. Not
that they said anything, but they're so damned self-sacrific-
ing. How can men bear to live like that? Poverty is something I run away from, but they go out of their way to
find it."

"They do good work," said Dumarest. He looked at
Vekta Gorlyk. "Don't you agree?"

"Yes," he said. "I agree."

His voice was flat, like his face, devoid of expression, a
dull monotone which gave no added emphasis to his words.

Dumarest said, watching, "You don't find many in this
part of the galaxy. Not like you do in the Center. But
there seem to be plenty of cybers about, and that's odd
when you think about it. If the Cyclan is established out
here, then why not the Church? You have an opinion?"

"I haven't thought about it. I don't travel much. I
wouldn't have noticed."

"Cybers go where the money is," said Chom. "Money
and influence. Those who aren't welcome in high places
wouldn't see them. What's your trade, Gorlyk?"

"I am a dealer in rare and precious books."

"Books!" Chom raised his eyes and shrugged. "And who
buys those? Museums and libraries and eccentrics. You
could trade for a lifetime and never see a cyber. Now if
you were like Earl here, a man who gets around and
moves high, then you would. Well, let's get on with the
game. Daroca?"

"I'll stay."

Dumarest sat back as the play went its course. Chom
spoke too much of things he could only assume and he
wondered at the entrepreneur's reason. Envy, perhaps? It
was logical, yet somehow it didn't seem to be the answer.
A man in his profession would have early learned the
value of silence. It almost seemed that he was advertising,
warning, even, but why and to whom?

He looked again at Gorlyk, studying, judging. The man
had certain disquieting characteristics. His emotionless im-
passivity, the dull monotone of his voice, his precision
even. A cyber could feel no emotion; an operation per-
formed at puberty divorced the brain from all physical
sensation so that he was a stranger to hate and fear, pain

and envy. Food was a tasteless fuel, the rarest wine less
commendable than plain water. They were living machines
who could never experience love and whose only pleasure
lay in mental achievement. The knowledge that the predic-
tions they made extrapolated from available data were
correct.

Dumarest felt an awareness of danger. If Gorlyk was a
cyber in disguise, divorced from his scarlet robe, his
shaven skull covered with a wig or natural hair, then the
Cyclan knew exactly where he was and where he was
going. And that was the one thing he had done his best to
avoid.

Daroca looked up from his cards as footsteps sounded
down the passage outside. He frowned as others followed,
their vibration loud in the silence of the salon. "Something
odd," he said. "Trouble, perhaps?"

"That bitch has seduced the crew and they're after her."
Mari was contemptuous. "Forget it. Deal, Harg."

"Something's wrong," said Chom. His voice reflected his
fear. "The engines, perhaps?"

"If they go you'd never know it," said Mari. "You'd be
dead." She cocked her head, listening, then rested her ear
against the table. "There's a lot of noise somewhere," she
reported. "I can pick it up loud and clear. Sounds like a
fight of some kind."

Dumarest followed her example. Transmitted by the
metal structure he could hear thuds and what seemed to
be shouting. As he rose the door of the salon burst open
and a uniformed man came inside.

Officer Karn did his best to be casual. "Harg," he said.
"You're wanted in the hold. Quickly."

The gambler made no move to obey. "That isn't my de-
partment."

"Captain Seleem gave the order. If you want to ride on
this ship again you'd better do as he says." His calm broke
a little. "Damn you, don't argue with me. You're wanted
in the hold. Now move!"

Reluctantly Harg threw down his cards and headed
toward the door. As he opened it the distant sounds became louder. Dumarest caught the officer by the arm as
he was about to leave.

"What's wrong?"

"Nothing that need concern you. If you will all stay in the salon you'll be quite safe. Unless—" He broke off, studying Dumarest, his height, the sheer gray of his tunic and pants, the high boots and the hilt of the knife riding just below his right knee. "I can't demand this," he said. "But we're short of men. If you could help?"

"What needs to be done?"

Outside, walking down the passage, the officer explained. "Some fool bribed the handler and got into the hold. We're carrying a beast for the zoo on Selegal. Because of its peculiar metabolism it couldn't be frozen, so we held it in a cage. Somehow it broke free. Now we're trying to get it back."

Dumarest listened to the noise. "An animal?"

"You haven't seen it yet," said Karn grimly. "Wait until you do."

Seleem stood outside the closed door of the hold, Harg and the steward beside him together with two other officers. They carried ropes and nets and the steward held a hypogun. The captain nodded to Dumarest as Karn explained why he had brought him along.

"Thank you for offering to help. We need all we can get. You know what happened?"

"I can guess. Bitola and the girl?"

"Her guard too. The girl managed to get out, not the others. She was hysterical and I've got her safe in her cabin, asleep." He glanced at the instrument in the steward's hand. "Have you trapped game before? Good. You probably know more about it than any of us. Can you give us some advice?"

"Keep clear," said Dumarest. "Move fast, don't hesitate and don't fumble. How big is this thing?" He frowned at the reply. "That big? And fast? There are enough of us for three teams. I'll go with Harg, Karn with the steward, the two officers together. Approach it from three directions. It can only move in one direction at a time and, when it does, the other two teams move in with the nets. Muffle it, rope it, hold it fast. And hold it," he emphasized. "Weaken and it will break free."

"Three teams," said Seleem. "Six men. What do I do?"

"You've got a ship to run. If we don't make it you'll

have to laser it down." Dumarest glanced at the steward.
"Let's get on with it."

The hiss of the hypogun as it blasted drugs into his
bloodstream was followed by an immediate reaction.
Dumarest drew a deep breath as the neutralized quick-
time ceased to affect his metabolism. The lights bright-
ened, the noises from beyond the door slowed so that he
could determine the sound of metallic crashing, the shatter of crystal, a solid, repetitive thudding. Gently he took
the instrument from the steward's hand, careful least he
should bruise flesh or break bones. Like the others the
man stood as if made of stone. He shook himself as
Dumarest fired at his neck, the others treated before he
could completely recover. They tensed, nets and ropes in
hand, ready as Seleem opened the door.

Inside lay chaos.

The caskets had been smashed, the wiring, the lights
and metal plating. Blood spattered the gleaming fragments
and a shapeless something lay before a twelve-foot cube
of thick bars. The handler, Dumarest guessed, or the
guard or even Bitola, but he wasted no time making certain. The broken lights had robbed the place of illumination, only a single tube casting a glow over the cage, the
rest in crawling shadow.

From behind came Harg's strained whisper. "Earl?"

"Wait."

To walk into danger was worse than stupid. Before he
entered the hold Dumarest wanted to locate the beast. He
stared into the shadows, wondering where it could be. The
thing had sensed their approach, or it had caught the light
streaming through the open door, and it had stilled all
movement.

"Get something heavy," he ordered. "Throw it past me
into the hold. Hurry."

He heard Seleem grunt and then something flew past his
head to crash against the floor. In the shadows something
moved, a bulky shape, scaled, legged, gem-like eyes in a
circle around a pointed head.

Dumarest lunged into the compartment, Harg following,
the others spreading to face the beast. As it sprang into
the light from the open door it stood fully revealed.

It was taller than a man, the head elongated into a sav-

age beak and mounted on a prehensile neck. The body
was like a pear, rounded at the base and ringed with
clawed legs. At the height of a man's waist smooth tentacles hooked, the ends split into finger-like appendages, circling the body. The eyes were set in circles of bone and
stared in all directions.

"God!" Harg sounded as if he were going to be ill.
"What kind of thing is that?"

An offshoot of evolution, the result of wild mutation,
that or perhaps it was perfectly fitted to its natural environment, Dumarest neither knew nor cared. He cried a
warning as light glinted on the shifting scales, the words
drowned in the sudden scrape of claws on the metal floor,
and one of the officers screamed as the pointed beak
ripped out his life.

"In! In, damn you!" Dumarest lunged forward, the net
streaming from his hands. It settled on the lifting head,
was ripped to shreds by the hooked tentacles. Before other
nets could join the first the thing was free and rushing
again to the attack.

This time the steward died.

"Get together," shouted Dumarest to Karn and the remaining officer. "Spread the net between you. Harg, grab
hold." He flung the end of a rope toward the gambler.
"Now run past it. Move!"

He raced toward the door, Harg running twenty feet to
one side, the rope stretched between them, the beast in the
middle. The rope hit, held, and, still running, the two men
passed in a circle about the beast, trapping it in another
loop of rope.

"Hold it!" Dumarest ordered as the beast lunged against
the restraint. "The net, quick now!"

He hauled as the beast moved toward Harg, white-
faced, sweating with terror. His boots slipped on the blood
staining the floor and the gambler yelled as a tentacle tore
at his sleeve, ripping the fabric from his arm and raking
an ugly gash down his bicep. Dumarest ran to one side,
rested his boot against the edge of one of the shattered
caskets, and heaved.

Harg released the rope.

The thing came like a thunderbolt, a waft of sickening
odor and a blur of lashing tentacles. Dumarest staggering

back, off balance with the sudden release of tension, felt the hooks tear at his chest, the clawed feet at his stomach and legs. He dropped the rope and flung himself aside as the vicious beak dented the metal where he had stood. Blows stung his back as he rolled, regaining his feet just in time to avoid the thrusting head.

Automatically his hand fell to the top of his boot, and lifted the knife, its razor edge catching the single remaining light.

Seleem, from where he stood in the open door, yelled, "Don't kill it!"

Dumarest ignored the command. He was fighting for his life, blocking the lash of tentacles with his left arm, the knife in his right slashing, cutting, lopping the ripping hooks, stabbing at the circle of eyes. Green ichor spattered his face, his head, stinging as it touched the naked flesh. He backed away, wary for his eyes, chest heaving, body in a fighter's crouch.

"Don't kill it!" shouted Seleem again. "Karn, Grog, get it!"

They ran forward with their net as the beast lunged toward the open door. It had been attracted by the captain's shouts, the blaze of light and, perhaps, the possibility of escape. Karn fell aside, one hand to his face as his companion doubled, screaming, hands clutching his ripped stomach.

Too late Seleem tried to close the door. The beast hit the closing panel, threw it back against the captain, slamming him against the wall. Dumarest followed it into the engine room, saw it lope toward the massive bulk of the generators. The pointed head darted forward, the beak slamming against the metal cover. It boomed, dented, but held. Again the head slammed forward. A third time.

"The engine!" Seleem staggered from where he had been crushed. "Stop it!"

Dumarest lifted his knife. His arm swept back, forward, the blade a glittering icicle as it left his hand. It struck the beast just below the circle of eyes and buried itself to the hilt. The thing reared, pointed head lifting, and from the open beak came a deep, gurgling ululation.

Then the head slammed down again, the beak ripping through the plating, burying itself in the mass of delicate machinery beneath. Fire blossomed around it, a gush of released energy, searing, incinerating, filling the compartment with the stench of roasting flesh. It spread, melting the casing, the carefully constructed parts inside.

"God!" whispered Seleem. "The engine!"

It had died, as the beast had died, as they would all die unless it could be repaired.

Chapter

◆ **THREE** ◆

Karn had entered the engine room, the gambler at his side. They watched as Dumarest walked to the dead creature and tugged his knife free. The blade was warm to the touch and stained with the acid ichor. He wiped it on his tunic and replaced it in his boot.

"Help me get this thing clear of the generator," he said. "Make sure the power is disconnected."

Together they lugged it from the ruined machine and dropped it against a wall. It was heavy for its bulk and death had coated it with a nauseous slime.

"It's dead," said Seleem. He seemed to be numbed by the loss. "I was to be paid on delivery and there's a penalty clause. I'll be ruined."

Shock and injury had disturbed the balance of his mind and he sought refuge in comparative trivia.

"I told you not to kill it," he said accusingly. "I warned you that it was something special. How am I going to meet the penalty? A lifetime in space," he mourned. "Twenty years as a captain. Five as an owner. Now I'm finished. You shouldn't have killed it."

"I didn't," said Dumarest.

"You could have," said Karn. The blood on his face gave him a peculiar, lopsided appearance. "I've never seen anyone move so fast. For a moment there I thought it had you, the time when Harg let go of the rope, but you managed to move out of its way. And when you fought it!" He shook his head, doubting what he had seen.

Harg said, "Earl, about that rope. I couldn't help it. The pain got me and I couldn't hold it with one hand. I'm

26

sorry, but I just couldn't hold it. You've got to believe that."

"He believes it," said Karn. "If he didn't you'd be dead by now." He kicked at the dead beast. "Damned thing. Three good men gone and all because some stupid bitch had to be clever. She must have opened the cage for some reason and look what happened."

"No," said Dumarest. "She didn't open the cage."

"Her friend, then. It's the same thing."

It wasn't that either, as Dumarest had known from the first. He glanced at Seleem, still trembling, then at the ruined generator. It presented no great urgency; if it could be repaired a few hours wouldn't matter, if not, then time was of no importance.

"Let's go back to the hold," he said. "There's something I want to see."

The shambles seemed worse than before now that the need for violent action was past. Dumarest stood looking, checking, verifying his suspicions. The dead officers and the steward lay where they had fallen. The handler was a shapeless huddle before the cage, recognizable only by his tattered uniform. Bitola was close to the door, the amazon sprawled even nearer and a little to one side. Her face was badly ripped and the beak had smashed her chest, but her expression was recognizable. Determination. She must have thrust her charge through the panel, slammed it, and turned to face the beast. Or perhaps the girl had been given time to escape and had closed the door herself. Now it didn't matter.

But she and the others had been on quick-time and it would have been impossible for her ever to have moved fast enough had she been near the cage when the creature broke free. They must have been leaving, actually at the open door, when it had attacked.

To Seleem he said, "What did they tell you about the beast? The shippers, I mean. Did they warn you it was intelligent?"

"No." The captain looked at his trembling hands. "They said it was just an animal. Something for the zoo. It couldn't be frozen or given quick-time. They supplied it in the cage and all I had to do was to feed and water it at regular intervals."

Karn said, "What are you getting at, Earl?"

"The shippers lied. That thing was more dangerous than they told you. Or perhaps it underwent a metamorphosis of some kind. What kind of lock was fitted to the cage?"

"It was simple enough. A pressure plate which had to be pushed and then slid to one side and then down. An animal couldn't figure it out unless—" He paused and then added, slowly, "I see what you mean. The damned thing must have let itself out and it couldn't have done that unless it had intelligence of some kind. But what was the point? I mean, if it was intelligent, surely it would have known there was no possibility of escape."

How to tell the workings of an alien mind? And yet some things were common to all life forms. Dumarest looked at the smashed caskets, the broken lights, the dark corners in which things could safely lurk.

He said, "The beast could have been a gravid female. It may not have wanted to escape as we use the term, but to settle its young."

"Hell," said Karn. "That means we have to search every inch of the hold. Now?"

"You saw the big one. We don't know how fast they grow."

"Now," decided the officer. He frowned, thinking, his hand touching the dried blood on his cheek. "I'll fix some lights and get some help. This is an emergency and the passengers will have to cooperate. Captain?"

Seleem winced as he drew in his breath. He seemed to have recovered his full awareness, probably helped by the knowledge that, as the shippers had failed to give due warning as to the intelligence of the beast, he was no longer responsible and no longer liable to the penalty he had agreed to pay for failed delivery.

"Do as you think best, Karn. My chest hurts, my head. I took a beating when that thing slammed me against the wall. And we've lost too many men. There's only you and myself left now." He looked at Dumarest. "How about you? Have you worked on ships before?"

"Yes."

"I'm needed at the controls. We both can navigate and Karn knows something about engineering, but we need someone to take care of the passengers. As from now you're my third officer with pay starting from the time we left Frell. Your passage money will be returned. Agreed?"

"Agreed."

"I'll need you all to sign a deposition as to what happened, but we can do that later." Seleem took a careful breath. "Now I'd better get back to the control room. Karn, keep me informed."

"He's hurt," said Dumarest as the captain moved slowly away. "He could have cracked ribs and maybe some brain damage. Have you a medic on board?"

Karn looked at the crumpled body of the steward. "We did, not now. Suggestions?"

"Mari Analoch might know something about medicine; get her to look at the captain. The Qualish brothers are engineers; they can start work on the generator. Gorlyk and Harg can help me to search the hold while you check for life-support damage. Right?"

"Right," said Karn. "You know, Earl, you're going to make a damn fine officer."

Mari Analoch said, "You're a fool, Earl. I heard all about it when I fixed up Karn and the gambler. Why the hell didn't you run when you had the chance? Fighting that thing the way you did. It could have ripped your face and taken out your eyes. I don't like to see a good man wasted."

She sat on the bed in his cabin, a tray of medicants at her side, a sheet wrapped around the expensive fabric of her gown. Her hair was slightly disarranged and her cosmetics, untended, betrayed the age she fought hard to conceal. A hard woman, ruthless and practical, but she had volunteered to help.

"You shouldn't listen to gossip," said Dumarest. "And I had no choice. Had I tried to run it would have got me."

"So you say. Now get those clothes off and let me inspect the damage."

"Seleem?"

"He's all right. A couple of cracked ribs and slight concussion I put him under slow time and he'll be fine in an hour."

She watched as he stripped, the protective mesh buried in the plastic of his clothing glinting as it caught the light through the scarred material. It had saved him from the ripping hooks and claws, but though it had withstood penetration it had done little to nullify the whip-like impact of the blows. The hard, white surface of his skin was striped and marred with purple bruises, his left forearm a mass of welts.

And, clear against the skin, sharp against the bruises, were the thin cicatrices of old wounds.

"Lie down," she ordered. "On your face." Lotions stung his back and brought a soothing numbness. "You're a fighter," she said, and he could feel the tip of her finger as it traced the pattern of his scars. "Ten-inch blades and the winner take all. Right?"

She grunted as he didn't answer, moving down his body, the swab in her hand moving over his hips, his legs.

"Turn over. Are you ashamed of it?"

The light was behind her, limning her hair with a halo of brilliance, casting her face in shadow and softening her features so that, for a moment, he could see something of what she had once been. Young and soft with a determined line to the jaw and lips which could smile, but rarely with her eyes.

"No," she said. "You're not ashamed. You're like me, doing what has to be done and making the best of it. A girl can't fight in a ring, but she can get by in other ways. A man now, that's different. The ring takes care of the weaklings." The swab moved over his chest and down to his stomach. "The ring," she said. "I've watched a thousand fights, but I could never understand why they do it. For money, yes, that I can appreciate, but why else? Do you get a kick out of it? Is it fun to kill a man? Some say it is. I don't think you're one of them."

The swab moved lower, passed over his loins, moved without lingering to the tops of his thighs. He relaxed, thinking, remembering. The blood-hunger of the crowd, the eager anticipation of blood and pain, the shouts and yells and the stench of sweat and fear. The grim knowledge that it was either win or die or, if not that, to be slashed and cut for a savage holiday. And, always, the conviction that luck could not last forever, that a single slip, a mistake, a patch of blood beneath a foot, the sun reflecting from a polished surface, anything, could tilt the balance and defeat all skill.

"Earl?"

He realized that she waited for an answer.

"Do you, Earl? Fight because you like it?"

"I fight only when I must." He was curt, not wanting to discuss it. "Have you finished?"

She was in no hurry, admiring the shape of him, the firmness, the touch of his skin as she let her fingers trail over the edge of the swab. Any woman could be happy with a man like this, and she wondered why he traveled alone. Not for the want of opportunity, of that she was convinced. Old and cynical as she was, yet even she could feel herself respond to his nearness. Had she been thirty years younger, twenty even—but it was useless to dream. The curse of her sex, she thought wryly. The biological need, not for passion, but to be with a man she could respect. The type of man she had never found—or had found too late.

"Mari?"

She had lingered too long, perhaps betrayed herself, and that was something she had never done before. Not even as a young girl, when she had first learned that what is said and what is meant are not always the same thing. She turned and dropped the swab into her tray.

"No damage," she said. "You'll be as good as new soon. Did you finish clearing the hold?"

Harg would have told her of the fifteen eggs they had destroyed, each as large as a doubled fist, each pulsing with life, but he told her again, not wanting to be hurtful.

"Seleem was a fool to have carried the thing," she said. "A bigger fool not to have sealed it in something solid. And insane not to have lasered it down at the beginning." She paused, then said quietly, "Just how bad are things, Earl? I would appreciate the truth."

"The hold is wrecked, Mari, but it can be repaired. I've got Chom and Gorlyk working on the caskets and Harg is rewiring the refrigeration units. Karn is confident that he can repair the generator. It's only a matter of time."

"And in the meantime we drift," she said shrewdly. "The field is down. Earl, why waste time repairing the caskets?"

"We have time. And it gives us something to do."

"To stop us thinking?"

She was too shrewd. The Erhaft field no longer protected or moved the vessel, and they were vulnerable to the hazards of space. Debris could impact the hull, a wandering meteor, even, rare, but always possible; a dozen things to threaten their lives.

"Suppose we can't repair the engine," she said thoughtfully. "What then? Do we drift until we die of old age? Or—" She broke off, frowning. The chance of rescue between the stars was so remote as to be inconceivable, but closer to a planet? "The caskets! Earl, do you think we'll have to ride Low?"

He smiled and shook his head. "You've too vivid an imagination, Mari. Anyway, would it be so bad?"

"I've done it before, when I had to, but twice was enough. And this would be different. We'd never know if we would be found. Damn it, Earl! I asked you not to lie to me!"

"I haven't lied." He reared up from the bed, his hands hard as they caught her arms, his face close to her own. "Listen, we hope to repair the generator. I'm sure we can do it, but only a fool takes no precautions. It may take longer than we know. All right; at the worst it may be impossible. But we still have a chance. In the caskets we can wait as the ship drifts to some habitable world when we can be rescued. That is why I am repairing the equipment in the hold. Now you know, but if you open that great mouth of yours and talk about it I'll close it for good. Get it?"

It was a language she understood.

Alone, Dumarest leaned back on the cot, closing his eyes and trying for sleep. He was overtense, the muscles jerking beneath his skin, his adrenalin-flushed blood denying relaxation. From somewhere came a thin, high keening, the Ghenka, he guessed, at practice or mourning the dead. Soon they would have to be evicted, the crewmen certainly, and he doubted if Lolis would want to have the body of her guard preserved for planetary burial. Bitola would go with the rest. A short, empty life quickly ended.

Well, perhaps he had been lucky. For him, at least, death had come quickly.

He turned, one hand by accident touching the metal bulkhead. The alloy was dead, lacking the faint vibration of the field, and he turned again, finally opening his eyes and looking at the ceiling. It was smooth, the paint fresh and bright. Seleem kept a good ship.

The keening rose, broke, then commenced again on a different key, a different song. It seemed louder than before and his mind began to fill with images, a woman with hair of spun silver and limbs of elfin grace. Another, this time with hair like flame and eyes of emerald. Kalin, who had given him so much. Whom he could never forget.

The song guided his thoughts in a chain of associated ideas. Kalin, and the secret she had given him; the Cyclan members who wanted to regain what had been stolen from their secret laboratory. The sequence in which the fifteen molecular units needed to be arranged to form the affinity-twin. Fifteen units, the last reversed to determine dominant or submissive characteristics. A combination which could be found by trial and error—given time. Too much time for the impatience of the Cyclan dedicated as it was to total domination of the galaxy. The possible number of arrangements ran into the millions; if it were possible to assemble and test one each second it would take four thousand years to try them all.

But, once found, it would give power incredible in its scope.

The artificial symbiote, injected into the bloodstream, would nestle in the base of the cortex and take control of the entire nervous and sensory system. The brain containing the dominant half would take over the body of the host. The brain of a cyber would reside in each and every person of influence and power. They would be puppets sitting on thrones and moving to the dictates of their masters. The Cyclan had once owned the secret, but now Dumarest had it, and the Cyclan would move worlds in order to recover it.

He had been forced to fight and run to keep it from their hands too often.

And, always, there was the danger that the Cybers' predictive skill had set a trap into which he would enter.

Gorlyk, perhaps?

He rose with sudden determination. If the man was working for the Cyclan there could be evidence in his cabin. He was working in the hold and it would be a simple matter to make a check.

Once dressed, Dumarest left the room and headed down the passage toward Gorlyk's cabin. The door was locked, but he had the steward's master key. Inside it was dark, the air heavy with a musty odor. Light blazed as he turned the switch and looked at the neatly-made bed, the cabinet, the piled suitcases, the small things a man carries to give him comfort and the illusion of home. A block of clear plastic held a single bloom of yellow laced with green, the styles a flaming scarlet against stamens of dusty black. A box of carved wood chimed when he opened the lid, a simple tune reminiscent of meadows and lakes. A string of well-thumbed beads, a tiny plaque bearing an abstract design, a bowl intricately decorated with women and beasts.

Souvenirs, perhaps. Little things collected during travel, or they could hold a greater significance to their rightful owner. A cyber would never have tolerated such emotional unessentials, but a cyber in disguise could have deliberately assembled them as a part of his deception.

Dumarest examined the cabinet. It held nothing but clothes, a single change of apparel together with a scarf of fringed and embroidered silk. The cases were heavy and locked with simple combination devices. He stooped, resting his ear against the mechanism, his fingers gentle as they turned the dial. A minute click, another, two more and the lid rose at his touch. Inside rested a heap of shabby books.

He lifted one, riffling the pages, smelling the odor of must rising from the volume. The paper was yellow and had obviously been treated with some form of plastic in ancient times, but the coating had worn thin and the revealed paper showed signs of decay. He had no idea as to the volume's value or worth. The title was in faded gold, tarnished, indecipherable. He looked again at the interior. The print was archaic and hard to read. He scanned half a page before deciding that it was some form of fictional romance. More deception? Or was Gorlyk exactly what he claimed to be?

He checked the rest of the contents, finding nothing except more books, replacing them as he had found them and closing the lid before spinning the dial. He looked under the mattress, ran the tips of his fingers along the frame of the cot, and searched the artifacts for signs of hidden compartments. A second case revealed no more than the first. The third held thin manuals dealing with mental disciplines, a large case of assorted drugs and several packets of dried vegetation. One of them seemed to be fungus of some kind, another a type of grass. Hallucinogens, perhaps? The basis of a health diet?

Dumarest replaced them and noticed a fold of paper protruding from one of the manuals. It was covered with a mass of neatly-written figures all in groups of seven. He turned it over and looked at the hatefully familiar tracing of the Cyclan seal.

Chapter

◆ FOUR ◆

Captain Seleem raised his cup of basic, drank and said thoughtfully, "Vekta Gorlyk? No, I have no personal knowledge of the man."

"Has he traveled with you before?"

"I think so. A few times, at least, but I cannot be certain as to the dates." Seleem drank again, emptying the cup. His eyes were bright and clear, but his face bore the marks of deprivation. Slow-time had speeded his metabolism so that he had lived days in an hour. Unconscious, he had starved. Had the treatment lasted longer he would have died. "You have a reason for your interest?"

Dumarest handed him another cup. "I was curious. He seems a strange person and I wondered if you knew anything about him. Where did he join the ship?"

"Phengala."

It was the world from which the ship had come to Grill, where Dumarest had joined it. It had gone then to Frell and had been scheduled to stop at Selegal and finally to arrive at Ayette. Then the ship would retrace its journey, serving a handful of worlds on a fairly regular schedule. There would be other ships each doing much the same. Did each carry a minion of the Cyclan?

Seleem moved cautiously in his chair. His brain was clear, but his chest still ached and when he breathed deeply he knew pain. Ribs took more than days to heal; he should take more slow-time and get himself fit as soon as possible. But first he had to restore his wasted tissues.

Dutifully he drank more basic.

"I've arranged a rota for the passengers," said Dumarest. "The men are doing what they can. Mari has taken over the steward's duties, and the Lady Lolis is still asleep. I've kept her under quick-time," he added. "The rest are normal."

"The Ghenka?"

"In her cabin. There is little she can do, but I will get her to relieve Mari when it becomes necessary."

Seleem nodded, appreciating the crisp report which gave information without a mass of trivial detail. But he had to be certain of one thing.

"Are you sure no trace of the beast remains? No undiscovered offspring?"

"We checked thoroughly. Nothing remains."

Seleem sat back in his chair and stared at the screens, the assembled instruments which ringed the control cabin. Normally those instruments would be busy, questing with their sensors, guiding the vessel through the immensity of space. They were still functioning as their power did not depend on the drive-generator, but now they were quiescent. Without the Erhaft field the ship was practically immobile.

Bleakly he stared at the stars revealed in the screens. They showed no sign of movement, appearing as static brilliant dots scattered thinly over the darkness, a smear of distant galaxies like a coil of gleaming smoke. A touch and the Center came into view, a host of suns each ringed by many worlds, curtains and sheets of light, great clouds of luminous gas, the whole interlaced with busy commerce. But here, where the stars were few and distances immense, ships were not plentiful.

"How long?" asked Dumarest.

"Until we reach Selegal?"

"There or somewhere else."

"Too long." Seleem was grim. "We have no velocity to speak of now that the Erhaft field is down. We are drifting at a fraction of the speed of light and the galactic drift makes a mockery of our original course. We shall arrive somewhere, given luck and sufficient time, but it could take centuries."

"Or never," said Dumarest.

"That is correct," said the captain. "There is no point in lying to you. Unless we are attracted by the gravitational field of some star we could drift for an eternity."

It was as he had known. Dumarest looked away from
the captain where he sat in his big chair, his face drawn in
the soft illumination from the screens. Seleem looked
older than he should, too old for his deprivation, his face
sagging with the inner knowledge of certain extinction
should the generator fail to be repaired. A red light shone
on one of the panels like a watchful eye. The possibility of
rescue was astronomically remote, but hope was eternal.
When the field had collapsed the automatic beacon had
begun to emit its call for aid.

The response was nothing but a thin wash of static, the
sounds of dying atoms carried on the radiation of space. It
was an empty sound, eerie, somehow frightening. The universe was too vast, too impersonal, and men were too
small and insignificant in comparison.

Randomly, Seleem touched a control, and abruptly the
sound changed. The thin, empty wash of spacial background noise became filled with a wailing lilt, crying, appealing, the sound of a soul in torment and carrying
within itself the epitome of abject loneliness.

"What's that?" Seleem's eyes darted about the control
room. "Dumarest?"

"Listen."

It came again, sobbing, a somber dirge of perfect harmony, rising to fall into pulsing tones, lifting again to a
crescendo.

"Something outside!" The captain reached for his instruments. His hand trembled as he made adjustments. "Loud
and strong and very close," he muttered. "But from
where?"

He glared at the screens, but they showed nothing new.
He adjusted them so as to scan the area all around the
vessel. Nothing.

"A malfunction, perhaps?" Seleem made rapid checks.
"No. Everything is in order. Someone is broadcasting on a
general band. Ultra-radio at high emission from a source
very close." He cut the volume and the wailing lilt faded
to a mournful echo. "What can it be?"

"It's the Ghenka," said Dumarest, listening. "It can't be
anything else."

He heard the song as he approached her cabin and wondered at the anguish it contained. He knocked and she fell silent as she opened the door and stepped back so as to allow him to enter her room. She had discarded her costume, the gems and paint, and now wore a simple dress of some clinging fabric. It rose high about her throat, full-sleeved, tight at the waist and falling to just below her knees. One side was slit almost to the hip to allow ease of movement. It flamed with a brilliant scarlet and, for a moment, he paused, half expecting to see a cowl, a shaven skull, the great seal he had reason to hate.

Then she switched on a brighter light and the illusion passed and he could see her as she really was.

A woman, no longer young, but not as old as he had suspected. Certainly not old enough to have run from competition, the wealthy worlds and rich patrons on which she depended. Her face was smoothly contoured, the mouth wide and generous, and what he could see of her throat was slender and unlined. Her hair was a rich bronze, closely-cut and fringed above the eyes. Her lips were full and soft, the lower almost pouting.

She inclined her head and said, "My lord, this is an honor."

"You know my name," he said. "Call me Earl. We have no need of formality."

"As you wish, Earl. My name is Mayenne."

"And you were singing. Why?"

"It is my trade. A skill must be practiced if it is not to weaken." She hesitated, then added, "And it gives me comfort. I am much alone."

Too much alone, he thought with sudden understanding. A toy to amuse the rich, an artist trapped by her training and achievement. Ghenkas were always remote and, on the ship, she had been mostly ignored.

Dumarest examined the cabin. The bed was unmarked, but the cabinet and small table were not as tidy as they could have been. A clutter of cosmetics, sprays, the gems she wore, all lying in a muddled heap. On the floor, fitted into a compact case, stood the familiar shape of an ultra-radio transceiver. Casually he picked it up.

"An unusual thing for a Ghenka to be carrying, Mayenne," he said. "A recorder I could understand, but why a radio?"

"It was a gift and it gives me comfort. With it I can listen to messages and music from many worlds. Surely there is no harm in a person owning a radio?"

"No harm," he admitted. "But to use it when there is no one to listen? You know our situation, girl. What did you hope to achieve?"

"Nothing."

"You sang into it just to amuse yourself?"

"Not to amuse. I was lonely and afraid and space is so empty. I hoped to pick up a message or some sign that we might be rescued. There was nothing but the sound of emptiness. It sounded so alone that I sang to comfort it. To comfort myself. Can you understand?"

Dumarest remembered the bleakness of the static he had heard in the control room, the eerie feeling it had created. It would not be hard for a person trained as the Ghenka had been in tonal efficiency to imagine the sound held words, almost recognizable, almost human. It was perfectly understandable that she could have sung back to it as a man might talk to a tree or to something which could not possibly answer. Loneliness took many strange paths.

He set down the radio and sat on the cot. "There is no need for you to be afraid. In a little while we will have repaired the generator and be on our way. On Selegal you'll make friends and no longer be alone."

"You are trying to be kind, Earl, but it will not be like that. It never is." She sat beside him, so close that he could feel the warmth of her body, the pressure of her thigh. "People do not accept me readily. Women hate me because of the influence they think I have over their men. Men desire me, not as a woman to be loved, but as a prize to be displayed. The rich are condescending and the poor are envious. Those who employ me try to cheat. Do you wonder why I need protection?"

"Guards can be hired and managers employed."

"You, Earl?"

He sensed the invitation, the unspoken offer of more than money if he agreed. The pressure of the thigh increased and the lips were close to his own.

Flatly he said, "No. I have other things to do. Perhaps Chom could help?"

"That man?" Her tone held a sneer. "He is an animal and a thief. Did you know that he tried to break into the dead man's cabin? I heard a sound and looked into the passage and he was trying to open the door."

"Bitola's cabin?"

"Yes. A short while ago. What else could he have been doing but seeking to rob the dead?"

It was possible and most likely true. The entrepreneur would not let such an opportunity pass, but Dumarest wasn't shocked and he doubted if the woman was either. They had both lived and learned the hard way. The dead had no use for their possessions, but the things they left could mean comfort to the living.

But, if she had seen Chom she could have seen his own search of Gorlyk's cabin. He thought about it, then decided against. Her door opened in the wrong direction; he would have seen the panel move. Yet was she all she appeared to be?

Would a Ghenka normally be carrying a high-powered ultra-radio of expensive make? A gift, she had said, but from whom? And why?

"You are troubled, Earl," she whispered. "Let me sing to you. Not all my songs are sad. I can create joy and passion and even forgetfulness. Listen!"

She began to hum, the soft tone rising, breaking into a ripple of cadences, words beginning to emerge, honeyed as they spoke of love and the satiation of desire. She caught his frown and, without breaking the song, immediately altered the pitch and rhythm, the words still soft and honeyed but now whispering of other things. Of home and a fire and the laughter of children. Of winds across an empty space and the triumph of growth. Another slight adjustment and he felt himself begin to sink into a reverie shot with mental images of an endless quest, of endless stars, of hardship and fulfillment to be achieved. And, always, beneath the words, the song, was the recognition of aching loneliness and the promise that it would be eased.

Unsteadily he said, "Enough, Mayenne."

Her hand touched his cheek, soft, gentle, the fingers trailing in a lingering caress.

"Earl, my darling. So long have I sought you. So much have I needed you. Do not leave me now."

He sank beneath the weight of her body and felt her warmth, her sudden hunger and consuming need. The scent of her perfume was a cloud accentuating his induced desire and his hands rose and touched the line of her back and shoulders, the helmet of her hair.

"Mayenne!"

The light died as she touched a switch and then there was only darkness, the lilting, singing whisper of her voice, the soft, demanding pressure of her silken flesh.

The bodies were gone, the mess, the smashed lights and crystal of the caskets. Even the floor had been cleaned of blood and ichor so that the hold seemed as if it had never witnessed pain and death and violent struggle. Dumarest raised a lid of one of the cabinets, sheet metal instead of the normal transparency, and felt the gush of frigid air rise from the interior. He closed the lid and switched on the mechanism, watching the temperature gauge as it fell. Satisfied, he moved to the others, testing each in turn. Again he moved down the line, this time checking to make sure the warming eddy currents were working at optimum efficiency. Finally he accepted the fact that the caskets, at least, were fully operational.

The generator was something else.

He paused in the engine room and glanced at the dismantled parts lying in neat array on the bench. Karn looked up from a sheaf of blueprints and nodded a welcome.

"Earl, satisfied with the hold?"

"It's as good as it will ever be."

"I wish I could say the same about this damned engine." The officer sounded as tired as he looked. Lines were graven on his normally smooth face and his eyes were sore, bloodshot.

Dumarest said, "Why don't you get some sleep?"

"Later."

"There's nothing that can't wait a while. Anyway, the Qualish brothers can handle things while you rest."

"They get on my nerves," said Karn. "They might be good engineers, but when it comes to repairing a machine all they can think of is replacements. Hell, to listen to them you'd think we had a factory just around the corner. They can't seem to get it into their thick heads that we have to make do with what we have."

"You're tired," said Dumarest.

"Sure I'm tired, but what has that got to do with it?" Karn shrugged as he met Dumarest's eyes. "So I'm being unfair," he admitted. "They aren't ship engineers and they can't help the way they think. And, from their point of view, they are right. The parts do need replacing. In fact we need a whole new generator and we'll get one as soon as we can—if we can."

Dumarest caught the note in the officer's voice.

"If?"

"It's bad, Earl. You're an officer now, so I'll give it to you straight. I think the Qualish brothers may have guessed, but they haven't said anything. If we get that generator going it will be a miracle." ·

"As bad as that?"

"I think so. Do you know anything about an Erhaft generator? They're factory-assembled and turned and they aren't meant to be torn apart. The worst that usually happens to them is that they get out of phase, but always there's a warning. Sometimes a ship is lucky to make a landing, but that's because some greedy captain pushes it hard and takes one chance too many. But that's about all."

Dumarest said, "Not quite. Sometimes an engine will fail."

"That's true," said Karn grimly. "But when it does no one knows anything about it. The ship just vanishes. Sometimes the collapsing field volatizes the structure; if it doesn't the ship just drifts until the end of time. We didn't volatize. One day, maybe, we'll form the part of another legend, a ghost ship which carries a crew of skeletons on a trip from nowhere to the same place. Something for people to talk about when they've nothing better to do. Hell, man, you've heard a dozen similar yarns in your time."

"Often," said Dumarest. "But we're not going to become one."

Karn made a sound deep in his throat. Fatigue and

despondency had colored his mood. He gestured to the dismantled generator.

"Look at it," he said flatly. "When that damned beast hit it was like shooting a bullet into a chronometer. The impact damage was bad enough, but when the energy went it really messed things up. We've stripped the whole thing and checked each part against the specifications. Most can be used, a few can be salvaged, but some will have to be replaced. Our spares are limited and will have to be adapted. The wiring is no problem and we can do something about the wave-guides, but the crystals are something else. From what I can see we are going to need three of them. They have to be the exact size, shape and structure. Tell me how to get them and I'll tell you when we can reach Selegal."

"Grow them?" suggested Dumarest. "Possible?"

"It's how they are made," admitted Karn. "But that would take equipment and measuring devices we haven't got. Try again."

"Is it possible to adapt or improvise?" Dumarest frowned, thinking, conscious of his lack of specialized knowledge. "An ultra-radio contains the same type of crystal, doesn't it? Would it be possible to assemble them in some way so as to regenerate the Erhaft field?"

He shrugged as he saw Karn's expression.

"I'm not an engineer and I'm shooting in the dark. I don't know what to suggest; all I am certain about is that, if you admit defeat, none of us has a chance. Now why don't you get some sleep? A tired mind is useless when it comes to solving a tough problem. You could make a mistake, overlook something, do irreparable damage." His tone hardened a little. "You put me in charge of the passengers, but you're as human as they are. Are you going to walk to your cabin or do I have to carry you?"

"Insubordination, Earl?"

"No, Karn, good sense and you know it. Now tell me what has to be done and then get some rest."

Karn sighed, admitting defeat. "All right, Earl, I'll do as you say. But if you can't find me those crystals there is only one thing to be done." He paused, then added softly, "You can pray. I can't think of anything else."

Chapter

◆ FIVE ◆

Lolis smiled and looked at the men gathered around the table in the salon, Harg, Chom, the silent Gorlyk. She breathed deeply, inflating her chest, conscious of their eyes. Chom purred as he gestured to a place at his side.

"Be seated, my lady."

Like the others he looked tired, worried, his eyes sunken in the puffiness of his cheeks. Against them Lolis was newly-risen, the effects of quick-time barely worn off, her eyes fresh and body relaxed from sleep and rest.

She said, "Where is Dumarest?"

"At his duties." Harg riffled his cards for want of something better to do.

"Do we need him, my lady?" Again Chom gestured his invitation. "I would offer you wine but things are not as they should be. Daroca has become morose and our new steward, or should I say stewardess, is careful of the supplies. But we have cards and conversation and they are enough to while away the tedious hours. Come, sit beside me and I will tell you of an adventure I had on a planet circling a triple sun. The girls held the power on that world and followed a strange courtship. I was younger then, and handsome in my fashion. I also owned jewels of rare value. Had I not been careless I might have ruled there yet."

He paused, waiting for her invitation to continue, but she had no time for boring reminiscences.

Harg said, "Your guard is dead, did you know?"

"And Bitola also." She was casual. "Yes, the old hag told me."

"And four other men," continued the gambler. "The

ship damaged and others hurt. Was it worth it to see the
beast?"

He was being unfair but her casualness annoyed him.
That and her arrogance. The incident was an unpleasant
memory, for her to be swiftly forgotten; her only regret
was at the loss of a servant and amusing companion. The
cards made an angry rasp in his hands. Perhaps, if he
could persuade her to play, some of the gems of which she
was so enamored would fall his way.

The prospect entranced him: to be rich, with money
enough to take up Mari's proposal, a half-share in a profitable enterprise. He could forget the acid taste of fear in
his mouth. He had been on spaceships too long not to
have recognized the danger of their position. The rest
might believe that all would be well, but he had seen the
captain and could read Karn's expression. A little more
luck, he prayed. One last safe planetfall, a little money to
see him through and he would be content.

He looked up as Mari entered the salon. She was
bedraggled, her hands showing marks of labor, and she
stood glaring at the girl.

"So you've finally decided to join us," she snapped.
"Didn't I tell you to start work in the kitchen?"

Lolis shrugged. "I am not a servant."

"And you think I am?" Mari fumed her temper. "Listen, girl; this is one time you have to earn your keep.
Things need to be done. The men want a soft bed when
they have finished their labors and they can't be expected
to prepare their own food and take care of their cabins.
So get to it."

"I am not a servant," repeated Lolis stubbornly. "And
how long does it take to prepare basic? How long to make
a bed?"

"Try it and find out."

"Not long," said the girl. "I have been trained in order
to maintain a palace. In my father's house the servants
were never idle. You are quite capable of doing what
needs to be done. And," she added with a sneer, "you
should be used to making beds."

"Bitch!"

"Hag!"

"By God," said Mari, shaking with rage. "If I had you

in one of my houses I'd take the skin from your back. I'd teach you manners, you chit. I'd have you crawl and beg forgiveness. I'd break your spirit."

"Mari!" Harg was concerned. Selegal was far from Ayette, but assassins could be hired and the girl was of the type to bear a grudge. "She is tired," he said to Lolis. "She doesn't mean what she says. You must forgive her, forgive us all. This has been a time of great strain."

"She is old," whispered Chom. "And jealous. You understand?"

It pleased her to be gracious. Smiling, Lolis said, "You have good friends, old woman. On Ayette I would have my husband teach you a lesson you would never forget. Now bring me food, quickly."

"When it is time."

"I said immediately."

She had gone too far. Lolis knew it as Mari advanced toward her, hands lifted, fingers hooked to rip at mouth and eyes. Her face had hardened into an animal-mask of sheer, vicious ferocity and the girl looked at death and worse than death, the ruining of the beauty of which she was so proud.

"No!" she said, backing away. "Touch me and I'll tell Dumarest."

"You think he'd care?"

"He loves me!"

The effrontery of it stopped Mari as nothing else could, turning her sudden anger into ribald amusement.

"You? A man like that in love with you? Girl, you dream."

"I saw him," said Lolis. "He looked into my cabin and I could read his eyes. Had I been fully awake he would not have left me."

She meant it, decided Mari. A twist of the imagination, a wish-image born of half sleep and boredom and perhaps a little more. He had rejected her, and such an unpleasant memory could not be tolerated. And so she had built a fantasy which fear and terror had brought into the open. That and perhaps something more. She wanted Dumarest to be in love with her so that, perhaps, she could take revenge for the imagined slight.

A child, Mari thought, *and I was going to treat her as I would a woman.* But even children had to learn.

Aloud she said, "Girl, you forget something. Days have passed while you were dreaming under quick-time. Earl is with the Ghenka."

"He wouldn't."

"Why not? Because you are a woman and you are here and, to you, no other woman could beat you at your own game? Earl is a man, child; what would he want with a stupid girl? The Ghenka wanted him and I think she is in love with him. He could be in love with her. Why not? They make a good pair."

There was a note of wistfulness in her voice, caught by Harg if no one else; then he saw the look in Chom's eyes and knew he wasn't alone. But the entrepreneur was subtle. Instead of the anticipated jest, cruel because of its truth, he said, "Mari, you are overtired. . . . My lady, the journey is not yet over and who can tell what tomorrow may bring? As every gambler knows, the one who wins today can lose all in a matter of hours. And," he added meaningfully, "few men enjoy the fruit which falls too easily into the hand."

The message was plain enough for even Lolis to understand. She was young, nubile, fresh, rich and lovely. Earl had taken what was at hand. Now, when he had a choice, he would be hers for the asking. And why not? With Hera safely out of the way, who was to bear tales? The entrepreneur could be bought, Harg threatened, Mari accused of spite and Gorlyk . . . ?

Deliberately she sat beside him and rested her hand on his arm.

"We have been strangers for too long," she murmured. "Tell me about yourself."

In the control room Seleem was dying. He sat slumped in his chair, face waxen, breathing shallowly, the air rasping in his chest and throat. Sweat dewed his features and Mayenne wiped it away with a scrap of scented fabric. He smiled his thanks weakly.

Dumarest stared bleakly at him, knowing there was nothing he could do. The internal injuries he had suffered had been more serious than they had imagined. Splintered

ribs, perhaps, lacerating the lungs. Or a ruptured spleen—
he had no way of telling. Slow-time had cleared his mind,
but it would take more than rest to mend his body.

"You must eat," said Mayenne to the captain. "Please
try to take something. Daroca has some food of his own
which could tempt your appetite."

"Later."

Helplessly, she looked at Dumarest. The subdued light
caught the bronze of her hair, filling it with little splinters
of brilliance so that she seemed to be wearing a helmet of
burnished metal. She had changed her dress, sensing, with
her womanly intuition, that scarlet disturbed him. Now
she wore a gown which matched the color of her hair. It
too caught the light, the glow and the starshine from the
screens, adding to the illusion that she was a warrior
dressed in glinting mail.

Dumarest said, "Captain, we need you and your skill.
You must take food."

"The philosophy of a traveler," Seleem said softly. "Eat
while you are able because you can never be sure when
the opportunity will arise again." He coughed with a liquid
gurgling and blood showed at his lips. "Later."

"Earl," whispered Mayenne. "Is there nothing we can
do?"

A doctor could have operated, repaired the broken
body and used the magic of slow-time to accelerate
healing, keeping the captain unconscious and artificially
fed. But Dumarest lacked the necessary skill and the ship
was not equipped for such treatment. The only thing he
could do, the normal practice in such cases, was to freeze
the captain in one of the caskets until they could reach
proper facilities.

But Seleem was needed at the controls. And the captain
refused to abandon his command. He said weakly, "Report on the condition of the generator."

"Karn has reassembled what he could. Now he and the
Qualish brothers are trying to find some way to replace
the ruined crystals."

"Karn is a good man," said Seleem. "Not as good an
engineer as Grog, but he will do his best."

"I know that," said Dumarest.

"A good man," repeated Seleem.

He fell silent, brooding, regretting past mistakes. He should have killed the beast instead of trying to recapture it. He should not have used so many of his crew. He should have run from the door or closed it earlier. He had been greedy and now he was dying and the ship was dying with him. They would all die.

Dumarest said, "Mayenne?"

"Yes, Earl?" She followed him as he moved toward the door of the control room. "Is there something you want me to do?"

"Stay with him." He glanced to where the captain sat facing his instruments, the screens. "Get him to eat. Keep him alive and, more important, keep him from dying before his time. We need his skills. If Karn ever gets that generator working he will have to stay by it. Seleem is the only navigator we have."

"I understand."

"Daroca has done his best, but Seleem seems easier with you. Perhaps you could sing to him." He paused and added, "Happy songs. He must be kept cheerful."

"All my songs are happy ones now, my darling." Her arms lifted, closed around his neck and pulled his face closer to her own. Her lips were soft and gentle, then firmed with rising passion. "I love you, Earl. I love you. My life is yours. Remember that."

Her life, her love—for what little time remained.

Dumarest closed the door behind him, his face bleak as he heard the wash of static from the radio, the empty, eerie sound. And then came the notes of her song, soft, warmly human, a mother crooning to her child, a woman to her lover. Comfort for the dying captain, his tormented mind eased with induced imagery.

He heard voices from the salon and glanced inside, seeing the gambler dealing cards to Chom, Lolis sitting close beside Gorlyk. Mari entered, bearing cups of basic. She saw him and called for him to enter.

"Food, Earl. Shall I take some to the captain?"

"Yes, Mayenne too. Has Daroca eaten? The others?"

"Daroca's in his cabin; he didn't want anything. I've attended to the Qualish brothers and the officer. Double rations; they need the energy." She handed him a steaming cup. "And so do you. Sleep too; you've been working too hard, Earl. Now sit and get that down."

Her voice was falsely harsh to cover her concern. He smiled and took the cup and sat close to the girl. Lolis glanced at him, then returned her attention to Gorlyk. Let him be envious, a little jealous, perhaps. Later she would make him her own.

"And you mean you can do that?" she said to Gorlyk with feigned interest. "Really train your mind so as to improve its efficiency?"

"Certainly. It is a matter of conscious discipline. For thousands of years men have known that, by mental exercise, they could control their metabolistic behavior. For example, I could thrust a steel rod into my flesh and I would not bleed, feel pain, nor would the injury leave any trace or scar. When I was very young I saw a troupe of entertainers at a fair. They walked on broken glass, pierced their flesh with needles, held their hands in fire. The sight intrigued me and I determined to learn their secrets."

"Fakirs," said Chom. "A trick of the mind."

"Mental conditioning," insisted Gorlyk. His voice had warmed from its normal dull monotone; now it held a trace of warmth and pride. "Rigorous discipline exercised over many years. The brain is everything, all else of minor importance. Emotion is wasted energy. To feel hatred or anger is a weakness. Such things are the result of glandular secretions and, by mental control, can be prevented."

Slyly Lolis said, "And love?"

"An emotion detrimental to mental well-being."

Chom laughed and said, "It is fortunate for you that your mother did not subscribe to your teachings. Right, Earl?"

Dumarest made no comment.

"Love is everything," said Lolis. "I can't imagine what life would be like without it. To train yourself to be an unfeeling machine." She gave an exaggerated little shiver. "Horrible!"

"But efficient," said Gorlyk. "Love is not essential to the perpetuation of the race. Parthogenesis or artificial insemination could take care of later generations and such births could be strictly controlled on the basis of mental attainment. Think of what such a system would mean. The race would constantly grow in mental prowess; only those showing the highest ability would continue their line. The rest would be eliminated from the genetic pool. It would mean the millennium."

"Or sheer, unadulterated hell," said Harg. "Surely life is a matter of variety? Your plan would make all men the same."

"No," said Gorlyk. He paused, searching for an example. "Take this ship. Men designed it, built it, sent it traveling between the stars. Now it is obvious that there must be an optimum design for a vessel based on its function and purpose. Over the course of time ships have become more or less standardized. Trial and error have resulted in a pattern which we all know. Not perfection, but a greater efficiency when compared to earlier models. If we do it with ships, then why not with men?"

"And women?" Lolis glanced at Dumarest. He was drinking his basic, apparently uninterested in the conversation. "Would you like all women to be the same, Earl?"

"In many ways they are," said Chom before Dumarest could answer. "In the dark, at least."

She ignored the crudity. "Earl?"

To Gorlyk he said, "Have you heard of the Cyclan?"

For a moment the man hesitated, a shadow in his eyes; then he said, "I am not sure of what you mean."

"The Cyclan is an organization like those you speak of. It is dedicated to the mind. Emotion plays no part in its dealings. I find it strange you have not heard of it."

"A dealer in books," scoffed Chom. "Where would he have met a cyber?"

A hundred places, perhaps, Dumarest thought. The goods he dealt in were rare and costly and those who would buy them would have money and influence. And he carried a tracing of their seal.

Dumarest said, "Gorlyk, have you ever met a cyber?"

Again he paused slightly before answering, as if he were considering his reply—or tailoring it to suit the occasion.

"Yes," said Gorlyk. "Once. I was most impressed."

Impressed enough to have fashioned his life on what he had seen? To have copied the seal which the cyber would have worn emblazoned on the breast of his scarlet robe?

It was possible and a cautious man would not have

given an outright lie to a simple question. But Dumarest did not press the point. There would be time for that later.

However, unless Karn could repair the generator, there would be no need.

Daroca called softly from just within the open door of his cabin. "Earl! A moment?"

He seemed no different than he had before. The somber clothing was neat and clean; his face was unmarked by worry or doubt. He stepped back as Dumarest entered the cabin, and gestured to a chair.

"Some wine?"

"No, thank you."

"This is a special vintage," urged Daroca. "Something which I would venture to guess you have never tasted before." He produced a bottle fashioned of ebon glass, the darkness flecked with crystalline shimmers. Into a pair of the iron-glass goblets he poured what seemed to be a flood of bubbles suspended in an amber fluid. "A novelty," he said, handing Dumarest one of the glasses. "A secret of the vintners of Hammashend. I think it will amuse you."

Dumarest looked into his goblet. The bubbles were of various colors, floating, lambent spheres, touching, parting, never breaking their individual boundaries. He sipped and felt a cool tartness. Again, and this time he felt a globule break against his tongue. Immediately his mouth was filled with the taste of honey.

"A host of different flavors, each trapped in its own liqueur," said Daroca. "No two drinks are the same. It adds a new dimension to a social grace." He paused and added, "And such things should be enjoyed before it is too late."

"You know?"

"Our position? Certainly. I would be a fool if I did not."

"The others?"

"The girl has no mind for anything but herself. Harg, like all gamblers, is a philosopher. Chom?" Daroca shrugged. "An animal who will fight to the last in order to survive. Gorlyk has his mental discipline." He smiled with quiet humor. "It will be interesting to see him put it to the test."

"And yourself?"

"I am not afraid to die. No," Daroca corrected, "that is not wholly true. I am afraid of the lost opportunities death will bring. The places I shall not see, the things I shall not do. Stupid, perhaps, but to me death has always represented unfinished business. I am a methodical man, Earl. More wine?"

"No."

"Later, perhaps." Daroca leaned back in his chair. "Of us all I would guess that our situation bears hardest on you. You are a man of action, used to making his own way and, in a sense, controlling his own destiny. Now there is nothing you can do but wait. How long, Earl?"

Dumarest shrugged. "Karn is doing his best."

"Which we both know isn't going to be good enough." Daroca sipped at his wine, looking surprised at the flavor he had discovered. "Roses," he mused. "Or, no, the essence of shleng. Interesting."

"You aren't going to die," said Dumarest. "The caskets are repaired and are waiting. When it is time they will be filled."

"So I have heard. No, not from Mari, but I guessed she knows. The brothers were talking, and I have my own intelligence. Why else should you have them made ready? However, Earl, what else is that but anticipating the inevitable?"

"You will be alive," said Dumarest harshly. "You will have a chance. We all will."

"A fighter," mused Daroca. "You never give up."

"No," said Dumarest. "I never give up." He rose from his chair. "Was that all you wanted to talk about?"

"Wait. You haven't finished your wine."

Dumarest looked down at the goblet. He didn't want the wine, novel though it was. He didn't want to sit and talk about what he already knew too well. Daroca was probably bored, but there were others with whom he could converse. And the cabin, with its soft furnishings, seemed to stifle, pressing close with its metal and plastic.

"Wait," said Daroca again. "Please sit and finish your

wine. And let us talk a little. About Earth," he added softly. "Terra."

"You said that you'd never heard of the place."

"I said that I'd never been to that world," corrected Daroca as Dumarest resumed his chair. "That is true; I never have. Does it really exist?"

"I was born there." Dumarest sipped at his wine and his mouth filled with a sharp astringency reminiscent of dust. "An old world, scarred by ancient wars, on which life is not easy. There is a moon, huge and silver in the sky. The stars are few, and ships rare. I left as a mere boy, stowing away, and I had more luck than I deserved. The captain was old and kind. He could have evicted me; instead he allowed me to work my passage. Later, he died."

He sipped again, remembering the endless journeyings, the strange worlds as he moved deeper and deeper into the Center of the galaxy. Always traveling, until he moved in regions where even the very name of Earth was unknown.

"You came from that world," said Daroca musingly. "Can't you get back? Haven't you the coordinates?"

"No."

"But surely they can be found? There must be records."

"No," said Dumarest again. "I told you, Earth is a world which has been forgotten. The very name causes amusement. No one seems to know where it is."

"A mythical planet," said Daroca. "Or one which is assumed to be a mythical planet. I went on a quest for such a world once. Eden. A planet of supposed beauty and eternal life. I actually found it, or a world bearing that name. Needless to say, it was not what legend implied. A harsh world with a peculiar race of introverted people with ludicrous claims. They insisted that all mankind had originated on their planet, that it was the source of every race on every world in the galaxy. An obvious impossibility. But Earth?" He shook his head.

"And Terra?"

"They are the same, you say? If so, perhaps I can help you. I have heard the name before. There is a cult which holds that, like the Eden I told you about, all life originated on one planet. They call it Terra."

"The Original People," said Dumarest.

"You know of them?" Daroca sounded disappointed. "I'm sorry, Earl. I thought I could be of help. It seems that you already know all I can tell you."

"Perhaps not. Do you know how to contact the cult? Where they are to be found?"

"No."

It was the answer he had expected, but Dumarest was not disappointed. Earth was close, of that he was certain. Clues won over the years had guided him to this sector of the galaxy, and it could only be a matter of time before he would know exactly where it was to be found. Clues won on Toy, on Shrine, on Technos and Dradea. The threads winding close with, perhaps, the final answer to be found on Selegal.

"You are fortunate, Earl," said Daroca softly. "I envy you."

"Why?"

"You, at least, have a reason for living. A goal at which you can aim. I—" He broke off, shrugging. "Well, never mind. But to drift is not always a pleasant thing. Shall we finish the wine?"

Chapter

◆ SIX ◆

Dumarest woke to a pressure on his shoulder and the sound of an urgent voice.

"Earl, darling! Wake up! Wake up, Earl!"

It was Mayenne. She lifted her hand as she saw his opened eyes and stood quietly beside the bed as he sat upright. He felt weak, disorientated, his head spinning with vaguely remembered dreams. Daroca had kept him talking, and he had lingered, sensing the other man's need of companionship. Had some of the globules contained hallucinogens? Damn the man and his exotic wine!

Mayenne said, "Please, Earl. Hurry."

"A moment." He rose and rinsed his head, the cold water helping to wash the cobwebs from his brain. While dressing, he said, "Seleem?"

"He isn't dead, Earl, but something has happened to him. I went to the salon to prepare him some food, and when I returned he said that he'd heard voices."

"Voices? Another vessel?"

"I don't know."

"Did you hear them?"

"No. Earl, he looks so strange. He kept asking me if I could hear anything and I couldn't. So I came for you."

Seleem turned as they entered the control room. The lights were out, the chamber lit only by the telltales and the starglow from the screens. He was upright in his chair, eyes bright, shoulders squared as if his body had summoned up a reserve of energy.

"Dumarest," he said. "Check the screens. Negative?"

"Negative."

"Yet there has to be something out there. I heard it. Listen."

He touched a control and the thin wash of static poured into the room.

"Negative," said Dumarest. "Captain, maybe you'd better let me give you something."

"I'm not mad," snapped Seleem. "And I'm not suffering from delusions. I tell you I heard something."

"Voices, Captain? A response to our beacon?"

"No, not voices. It was more like a song. A sound like the girl makes. You remember? We heard it once together."

When she had sung into her radio and broadcast her voice to the stars. Dumarest met her eyes.

"No, Earl. I wasn't responsible. I swear it."

"But you were singing to the captain."

"Yes, but I'd left to get him food. There it is." She pointed to an untouched cup of basic standing on the chair-table. "I didn't sing and I didn't broadcast. You have my word for that."

A delusion then, the crying need for Seleem to save both himself and his command, causing him to fit imagined words to the empty static. Dumarest drew a deep breath, knowing that he had been a fool to hope.

"I heard it," insisted the captain. "It came loud and clear. I couldn't have been mistaken."

Dumarest said, "Mayenne, do you remember the song you sang before you went to get the food?"

"Yes, Earl."

"Sing it again."

"Now?"

"At once, Mayenne. Please."

He watched as the notes soared around him, filling the cabin, merging with the background wash of static. Seleem gave no response, sitting as before, and the telltales remained quiescent. A forlorn hope, but it had to be tried. At times ultra-radio had freakish ways, and, if nothing else, it would prove by negative response the captain's delusion.

Seleem stirred as Mayenne fell silent.

"It was something like that," he said. "Not exactly the same, but something—"

The radio burst into life.

It was a reflection, thought Dumarest wildly. A return

of what had been emitted, bounced back from some scrap of cosmic debris. Crystals, perhaps, vibrating in sympathy and rebroadcasting what they had received. And then he noticed the subtle differences. The song was not exactly the same: not even a mirror-image. It was as if someone had heard a shout and answered it with a blast of similar sound.

"There!" Seleem was trembling. "I told you I heard something! I told you!"

"Sing again," Dumarest ordered. "Use sequential notes in varying series and pause between each group."

"Earl?"

"Do it!" Urgency sharpened his voice, making it hard. "Aim for a response. If it is identical, it could be a reflection. If not, it could be the result of intelligence. Hurry."

He timed the song, the answer, checking and testing as Seleem adjusted his controls.

"Too low," he said after a prolonged space of silence. "Higher? Sing higher!"

The girl had a tonal range more than twice that in normal use. Her voice was a trained instrument capable of delicate variation and pure harmony. A Ghenka could smash glass and curdle milk, kill bacteria even, with the power of her voice. Dumarest felt the ache in his ears as her tones soared, saw the captain's eyes become suffused with blood and felt the thin vibration of the control panel on which his fingers rested.

"Enough!"

Tensely he waited for the response. When it came, there could no longer be any doubt. It was not a reflection.

Dumarest spoke into the radio. "This is a ship in distress. Do you understand? We are damaged and without motive power. We need assistance badly."

Nothing. The screens remained empty, the radio silent. Seleem stirred fretfully in his chair.

"Try again," he urged. "Dumarest, there's a ship out there somewhere. We've got to remain in contact. Try again."

"We don't know that it is a ship," said Dumarest. "All we can be sure of is that something, somewhere, is emitting a signal." He boosted the radio to the limit of its power. "Listen," he said harshly. "You out there, *listen*.

This is a ship in distress. We have suffered damage and are drifting. Unless we get help, we'll all die. Locate our position and come to our aid. *Quickly*. We have no time to waste."

Again no response.

"I don't understand this," muttered Seleem. "It answered the girl, why not you?"

Pitch, frequency, perhaps even the casual dictates of curiosity, how could they tell? Dumarest caught Mayenne by the arms.

"Sing to it. Attract it. Bring it to us, somehow. I don't know how," he said as he saw the question in her eyes. "But it answers you, and that is enough. Call to it, girl. Bring it close."

"But, Earl—" Her hand rose and touched her throat. "For how long must I sing?"

Even a trained voice had its limitations. Dumarest checked the panels, found the recorder and switched it on.

"As long as you can," he said flatly. "And then we'll use the tape. Now, Mayenne."

Karn entered the control room as she began. He stood, listening, as she sang for her life, the lives of them all. Her voice rose in a plaintive wail, shrilling, sobbing with a terrible yearning, calling, pleading in the universal language of despair.

As she paused he said, "Captain, I—"

Seleem cut him short. "Be quiet. We are in contact with something. Listen."

The song rose again, a little different than before, but still tearing at the nerves with the same impact. Karn felt a bleak helplessness, a fury at unresolved suffering and pain, a burning determination to help and aid whenever the opportunity arose.

The answer came in a roar of sound.

It blasted from the radio, lilting, wailing, seeming to hold a question. Dazed, Dumarest flung his hands to his ears. Karn caught Mayenne's look of anguish and heard Seleem's cry of pain. Then the sound changed. Now it no longer posed a question, but held decision.

The ship moved!

On the screens the stars shifted, flickered and were replaced by others, sparse and dull against the sky. A handful of somber points were backed by unending darkness, broken only by the smears of distant galaxies.

A world hung before them.

Seleem cried out and flung his hands at the useless controls. Dumarest caught a glimpse of harsh roughness, of rounded nubs which could once have been mountains, and then they were closer, hurtling toward a deep valley barely visible in the weak light of the stars.

"Earl!"

He heard the cry and felt Mayenne grip his arm. He caught her to him, cradling her tight, giving her the useless protection of his flesh as his skin crawled to anticipated destruction.

"Earl," she whispered. "Kiss me good-bye."

He felt the touch of her lips, the softness of her hair against his cheek, the warm pressure of her body as, helplessly, he waited.

And then, incredibly, the ship came harmlessly to rest.

"God!" Karn was sweating; his hands shook as he dabbed at his face and the trickle of blood from his bitten lips. "Landings like that I can do without. Are you all right? Earl? Mayenne?"

"Yes," she said. Like the officer, she was dazed. With her emotions set on approaching death she was slow to recognize the abrupt transition. Her eyes widened as they stared past Dumarest to the big chair. "The captain!"

Seleem was dead. He lay sprawled on the padding, blood edging his mouth, his eyes filled with the terror he had known at the last. Shock had sapped the remaining strength from his weakened body. Karn gently closed the staring eyes.

"A good man," he said bleakly. "And a damned fine captain. I know just how he must have felt. A dead ship and a certain crash. All he'd ever worked for on the edge of destruction and not a damned thing he could do about it. A hell of a way to end a life."

Dumarest said, "You're in command now."

"In command of what? A useless vessel stranded on an unknown world? You know why I came to the control room? It was to tell the captain that we didn't have a hope in hell of ever being able to repair the generator. I've tried everything I know and it isn't enough."

"It's still your command. And you have decisions to make, responsibilities. There are the passengers; have you forgotten?"

"No," said Karn. "I haven't forgotten. But how am I going to explain? One minute we were in space, the next . . .?" He shrugged. "What happened, Earl?"

"You saw it. You should know."

"Instantaneous transmission. I saw it but I still don't believe it. It goes against all the accepted laws of nature. The energy requirement alone would have been fantastic." Karn looked at the screens, at the rough terrain outside. To either side the cliffs framed a solitary star. "Something moved us," he said wonderingly. "Shifted us from where we were to where we are now. And where is that? Somewhere remote, that's obvious. We must be at the edge of the galaxy. But why?"

Mayenne said, "I called for help. Something answered."

"You call this help? The ship stranded and the captain dead?"

"That was an accident," said Dumarest. "He was ill, dying, and the strain was too great."

"So they couldn't help that, but why bring us here at all?"

Karn moved to the radio and boosted the gain. To the silence he said, "This is the commander of the vessel which has just landed. We are in distress and require immediate aid. Reply if you receive me."

He snarled at the lack of a response.

"Listen," he stormed. "You brought us here and you killed a man in doing it. Now talk to me, damn you. Talk!"

A rush of noise and then a single word came.

"Wait!"

Mayenne caught Dumarest's arm. "Earl! They answered! They can understand!"

"Then why don't they talk?" Karn adjusted the radio. "What are we supposed to wait for?"

"Wait," said the radio again. Then, in a disjointed rush, the voice said: " . . . Need to correlate data . . . communication . . . stimulation of reserve . . . unrelated form of reference . . . micro-currents of various transmitters oc-

cluded by engrossing irrelevancies ... time ... inconsistent
with ... manjhala hish ... secal. ..."

"Crazy," said Karn. "What's the matter with that opera-
tor? He doesn't make sense."

"He sounds so cold," said Mayenne in a whisper, as if
afraid of being overheard. "Like Gorlyk does at times.
Flat, dull, like a machine."

The radio emitted a series of clicks, a high-pitched whis-
tle and then a dull, rumbling grating sound which fell to a
sonorous booming.

"Damn you," said Karn. "You're getting on my nerves."
He glanced at Mayenne. "Perhaps she should sing to it
again."

"Use the tape," said Dumarest. "We recorded her last
songs."

It was worth a try and they had nothing to lose. As
Karn engaged the spool, he studied the screens. The edge
of the cliffs seemed a little different from what they had
been before, the bleak stone hazed with a mist of light. He
blinked, wondering if his eyes were at fault, but the soft
glow remained.

Karn rested his hand on the control. "Here goes.
Maybe, this time, we'll be sent back home. Right on the
field at Selegal would suit me fine." He froze as the radio
broke into new life.

"... compounded error ... communication by means of
vibrating membranes ... no ... vibration conducted
through gaseous medium ... no ... unessential ... signal
medium restricted to limited range of cycles ... correlate
with electromagnetic emissions ... malfunction. ..."

The cold voice held a frightening detachment. Dumarest
thought of a tiny insect lying on a path, a hand sweeping
it up and carrying it to a laboratory, there to mount it, ex-
amine it, perhaps dissect it. Would the creature comprehend the forces which had moved it? The musing of the
technician probing into its life?

"Earl," whispered Mayenne. "I'm afraid."

Had she grasped the analogy too?

Before he could ask, sound thundered around them: a
blast of noise so intense that it created physical pain. It
was as if the very walls of the vessel quivered to invisible

energies, vibrating in the aural spectrum, but so strongly that they could only cringe and wait for it to end.

"Stimulus inappropriate," said the radio. "Adjust."

Again the ship quivered with sound.

And the planet spoke.

It needed no mouth; mouths are only a means of vibrating gases. It needed no radio; it could control the passage of electrons, the emission of energies, as a part of its integral existence. All that was required was a diaphragm which could be vibrated within a range discernible to the ear. And the ear itself contained such a diaphragm.

To such a being it was a small thing to correlate words, to assign meanings, to construct the terminology and extrapolate from proven data. A man could do it, given time.

They could understand that. The sense of purpose and the taint of frustration was understandable too. Beyond understanding was the element of time.

It was old.

It had gained awareness and, inevitably, it had acquired an emotion. Just when it had made that acquisition had engrossed it for an eon during which suns had faded into embers and the area of space in which it drifted had become desolate and cold. The need for survival had driven it to regions where suns were hot and space full of needed radiation. But those suns in turn had died and again it had moved.

On such a scale time ceased to have meaning. The repetitive pageant had unfolded itself so often they were like the pages of a book; suns flaring to die, their planets disintegrating into dust; its own bulk maintained by manipulations of which it was a master.

It had crossed intergalactic space, a planet-sized intelligence which had been attracted by a song.

And it was bored.

Karn entered the salon and joined the others where they sat at the table, all congregating as if for mutual comfort and protection. There was no need for explanations; all had received the message. He nodded to Dumarest as he took a cup of basic from the tray which Mari had provided.

"I've taken care of the captain. Sealed him in one of the caskets for later burial. He'd want to be evicted into space, not planted in that thing out there."

"A worm," said Harg. "It made me feel about an inch high."

"But it can help us," said Lolis to Dumarest. "It can do anything. Surely you can make it repair the ship and send us on our way?"

"We can't make it do anything," he said flatly. "We can only ask."

"But you will do that?"

It was Karn's responsibility, not his, but he didn't bother to argue with her. Later they would ask. Later they would do what had to be done. But it would be at Tormyle's convenience, not theirs. Tormyle, the name the world had given itself.

Daroca touched Mayenne on the arm. "Perhaps if you sang to it again?" he suggested. "Bribed it, perhaps?"

Chom thoughtfully rubbed at his chin.

"You know, Earl, there are opportunities here. The thing must hold secrets of tremendous value. The way it shifted us, for example. If we could obtain such knowledge we could demand our own price."

He was serious, Dumarest decided. The man's natural defenses had narrowed his horizons to regions he could comprehend. To him the giant intelligence on which they rested was nothing more than a potential source of wealth. And he was right. The human mind could only grasp so much at a time. An enemy was no more to be feared because it was large. A virus could kill as surely as a planetary brain.

"I must talk to it," said Gorlyk. "I think you should elect me as your spokesman. I am the only one here with the training to deal with it. A machine must appreciate logical thought and I have devoted my life to perfecting mental discipline."

Karn said, "Why do you call it a machine?"

"Could it be anything else? No organic life could have lived for so long. Nor could it have grown so huge."

"It is bored," said Daroca. "Could a machine feel emotion?"

"A brain, to remain active, must be constantly supplied

with fresh stimuli," said Gorlyk. "To me it is self-evident that Tormyle cannot be the product of natural life. Therefore it must be a fabrication. Perhaps a self-perpetuating device of some kind."

"Not so fast." Sac Qualish stared down at his hands. They were rough, scarred with recent labor. "That thing comes from a long way away. We have no idea as to what life-forms are to be found in other galaxies. All we know is that it's bored and it wants us to provide intellectual stimulation. Can you do that?"

"Certainly."

"I couldn't." Sac glanced at his brother. "Could you, Tek?"

"No. I've been thinking about it and I know just how Harg feels. Like a child faced with a genius. A bug on a carpet waiting to be crushed."

Karn said, "It didn't say anything about intellectual stimulation. It just said that it was bored and hoped to relieve itself. That we would relieve it. Nothing was said as to how."

"What else could it be other than by mental stimulation?" Gorlyk looked around the table. "Do you agree I should be our spokesman?"

Chom said, musingly, "Not so fast, my friend. There could be certain advantages in being spokesman, but it would take a man used to devious ways to make the best of them. And not for himself alone, but for all. I am such a one. In my profession it is essential to have a ready tongue and nimble wit—two things you lack."

"Tormyle would not appreciate dealing with a liar and a thief," said Gorlyk coldly.

"You dare to call me that!"

"Your actions prove it. Shall I elucidate?"

"Shut up," said Harg.

"Our lives may depend on the correct choice. I insist on being the one."

"Be what you like," said Mari quickly. Nerves were taut and, like the gambler, she knew too well how soon a quarrel could become more vicious than words. "Just get us out of here and I'll give you a permanent free pass to any house I own. That's a promise."

"Don't be so free with what isn't yours to give," snapped

Chom. "I do not like to place my life in such hands. Earl?"

"Leave me out of it," said Dumarest.

"You then, Karn. You are the captain now. It is for you to make the decision."

"Toss for it," said the officer bitterly. "Or play cards. At least it will keep you from each other's throats."

"I'm willing," said Harg.

"I'm not." Daroca was firm. "Gorlyk is right when he says that our spokesman, should we need one, must be the best man available. Our lives could depend on the way he handles the situation. With respect to all present I submit that it should be either our captain or Dumarest. Karn will be needed to take care of the ship. Earl?"

"A good choice," said Mari. "You agree, Harg?"

The gambler nodded. Gorlyk said, "Why must the choice lie between them?"

"They are both officers," said Daroca mildly. "The only ones we have now. It could be that Tormyle will only have respect for established authority. I don't know, but officer or not, Dumarest is my choice."

Lolis said, "And mine. Earl, darling, you will agree?"

"I will think about it."

"And other things, darling?"

The invitation was plain, and he caught Mari's scowl, the sudden hardening of Mayenne's lips. But he was in no mood for the casual interplay of personal relationships. The girl was a fool and promised to be a nuisance.

Flatly he said, "My lady, you waste your time."

"Why, Earl? You go with the Ghenka; why not me? Am I so ugly?"

They were all under strain. A sharp retort would have been easy but unnecessarily cruel. Deliberately he softened his tone.

"You are very beautiful, my lady, as you well know. But you have much to learn." To Karn he said, "Captain, I think we should resume our watch."

The view had altered. There was a softness about the valley which had not been there before. Above, the single star winked and seemed to waver as they watched.

"Air," said Karn wonderingly. "But the planet is airless." He checked an instrument. "Three pounds pressure and rising. Earl?"

"It is making a place for us," said Dumarest. "An environment in which we can survive outside the ship. It has probably sealed the valley with force screens of some kind." He remembered the haze he had noticed earlier. "It could be manufactured from the stone, water perhaps, even food."

"Like God," said Karn wonderingly. "Creating a world to order."

Chapter
◆ SEVEN ◆

It was a paradise.

Dumarest stood just outside the open port of the vessel and breathed air which was rich and warm and filled with delicate perfumes. The valley was thick with exotic plants, bushes and flowering trees covering the barren harshness he remembered. Above the space between the cliffs was a shimmer of light as warm and as bright as any sunshine.

"It's beautiful," whispered Mayenne. "The kind of place I have always dreamed of. If I could live here, with you, Earl, I would want nothing else."

"It built well," admitted Karn.

Well and fast, using information taken from their own minds, Dumarest thought. He watched the others drift to either side, their voices clear on the scented air.

"A langish," said Daroca wonderingly. "I haven't seen one since I was a boy. They grow only in the foothills of the Jade Mountains on Klark."

Mari laughed as a fungus popped and released a cloud of spores to hang shimmering in the air.

Sac Qualish pulled golden ovoids from a tree.

"Taste this fruit, Tek. It's really something." He snorted as his brother hesitated. "Hell, if Tormyle wanted to kill us it wouldn't have to poison the fruit. Go ahead, there's nothing to worry about."

Karn said, "We should stop them, Earl."

"We can't, and Sac is right. I don't think we have anything to fear from the fruit and vegetation." Dumarest watched as Mayenne plucked a flower and held it to her nose. Pollen rose and she sneezed.

69

Lolis danced on a patch of lawn, blossoms wreathing her hair.

"This is wonderful," she called. "When I am married I will have a place built exactly like this. A love bower. Earl, come and join me. Let us explore."

She frowned as he made no move to obey.

"No? You then, Gorlyk."

"Wait!" Karn was unsure of himself, out of his depth and not knowing just what to do. "I think we should stay together. It wanted us outside; well, we are here, but maybe we should stay close to the ship."

"You worry too much," she called. "There's nothing to be afraid of."

Dumarest wished he could be as certain. He reached for a leaf and let it lie in his hand, not plucking it, holding it on its stem. Was it real or an illusion? The valley appeared to be a haven, but it could contain nothing except air. The rest might exist only in their minds.

He heard laughter. Lolis was dancing again, Gorlyk looking foolish in a lopsided garland of flowers which she had thrown over his head. The Qualish brothers stood beside the tree, their faces smeared with juice from its fruits. Mayenne was lost in a dream as she wandered, gathering flowers. Even Karn seemed to have relaxed.

He opened his blouse and bared his chest to the warmth of the sky.

"Paradise, Earl. The thing which people have looked for since the dawn of time. We could have found it."

"At a price."

"We can pay it. There are ten of us and between us we should be able to provide Tormyle with what it wants. And it can't be really bad, Earl. Would it have provided this garden if it was?"

A beautiful garden—if there was no serpent.

Dumarest felt the leaf quiver in his hand, vibrating, forming words.

As every leaf vibrated, so did the very molecules of the scented air.

"I am Tormyle."

It was a statement of fact as cold as ice and carrying the bleak detachment of a machine. Startled, they waited.

"You are sentient forms of life each containing an electromagnetic unit of intriguing complexity. Why do you not use it to communicate?"

"It's talking about our brains," said Karn wildly. "How can we answer that?"

Gorlyk took a step forward as if to attract attention.

To the air he said, "We are aware of our physical limitations. We are in the process of evolution and will, in time, be able to achieve mental communication. Now we use machines to obtain the same ends."

"Understood."

A silence and then Dumarest tensed as he felt the impact of invisible energies. A soft pressure enfolded his body, questing, probing before it vanished as suddenly as it had come. From their expressions he knew the others had suffered a similar experience.

"Soft," droned the air. "And different. You are of two kinds. Why is that?"

"For reproductive purposes," said Gorlyk quickly. He was determined to be the spokesman. "We represent both sexes. Male and female. The female bears the young." He added. "I am a male."

"Understood."

It was toying with them, Dumarest thought. Asking what it must already know. If it could have searched their minds in order to discover the things needed to fashion a suitable environment, then surely it must have gleaned other knowledge. And yet it was in the nature of a machine to verify all data. If it was a machine.

He said, "Will you repair our vessel?"

"Don't talk to it," said Gorlyk. "I am the spokesman. We agreed."

"Shut your mouth!" Chom snapped. "We aren't here to play games."

Dumarest ignored them both. He said flatly, "I asked you a question. Will you answer?"

The leaves rustled. "Dissension. A conflict of electromagnetic units. But there is more. I find it engrossing."

"Don't listen to him," said Gorlyk. "Tormyle, I am the one to whom you should speak."

"A metabolic alteration for no observable cause," said the air. "Increase in temperature and muscular tension. Some aberration of the cranial unit. Explain."

Anger, thought Dumarest. Gorlyk's training had let him down. He must be feeling rage at the interruption and overriding of his assumed authority. A cyber could never lose his temper. One minor problem, at least, had been solved.

Aloud he said, "He is feeling a strong emotion."

"Explain."

"He wants to hurt me. To destroy my function."

"Explain what you mean by emotion."

"A strong feeling caused by internal or external stimuli."

"Feeling?"

"Joy, hate, anger, love, fear, hope." Dumarest added: "I can't explain them. They have to be experienced. To the majority of our kind they make life what it is."

"Stimuli?"

"Opposition, possession, loss, achievement, failure, success." Dumarest paused. How to explain abstracts to something so alien? "I can't make it clearer than I have. You either know what I'm talking about or you don't. Obviously you don't."

The air stirred and Tormyle said, "Insufficient data to resolve unfamiliar concepts. Detailed examination essential before further progress."

Gorlyk vanished.

He went without trace, one second standing with his face turned toward the brightness of the sky, the next completely gone with not even a clap of air rushing to fill the vacuum he must have left.

Lolis screamed. "I felt it. Like a great hand snatching him away. I was standing right beside him and I felt it!"

"He must be somewhere." Karn ran to where he had been standing. The grass was unmarked. "Search," he ordered. "Spread out and look everywhere."

"No," said Dumarest. "It will be a waste of time. We all know what happened."

"Tormyle," said Daroca. "Do you think it is responsible?"

"You heard it. What else?"

"A specimen, snatched away for detailed examination." Mari dabbed at the sweat which had appeared on her face. "The poor devil. I never did like him, but at least he was human. Not like this." She stared uneasily at the vegetation shrouding the walls of the valley, its floor. "Perhaps we should get back into the ship."

It would make no difference and they found it impossible. The port had been closed and sealed. Like it or not they had to stay in the open; they clustered close at the base of the ramp.

Mayenne said, "Earl, what will happen to him?"

"Gorlyk? He will be studied."

"But how?"

"I don't know."

"Killed?"

Dumarest impatiently shook his head. Gorlyk was gone and it required little imagination to guess what would happen to him. Taken apart cell by cell, perhaps, tested and probed to destruction, torn apart in search of an elusive thing called emotion. Or perhaps Tormyle had more efficient means. Perhaps the planetary intelligence could test without destruction.

"It's watching us," Chom said broodingly. "I can feel it. Like spiders crawling on my skin."

"It's busy," Mari said shortly. "It's got no time for us at the moment."

"A brain like that could have time for a thousand things at once. Do you think it's as restricted as ourselves? And have you never done two things at the same time?"

"Yes," she admitted. "Often."

"And you have only a small brain," said Chom. "Think of what Tormyle can do. It's incredible."

He shivered a little and hunched himself small as if to escape the notice of a watching eye. It was a feeling they all shared. The primitive defense to cringe, to hide, to wait until danger had passed. But in this place there could be no hiding.

Dumarest said, "We had better eat. Let's gather fruits and see what else is available."

"You want us to go in there?" Mari jerked her head toward the undergrowth. "After what has happened?"

"You didn't want to search," reminded Karn. "You said it would be a waste of time."

"It would, and I'm not talking about making a search.

But we just can't sit here. Tormyle will do as it wants and there's nothing we can do about it."

"A philosopher," Chom sneered. "Well, Earl, this is something you can't tackle with that knife of yours. I suggest we find some way of buying our way out of here. Has anyone any ideas?"

Their voices blurred as Dumarest left the company. With Mayenne at his side, he headed into the underbrush. The bushes pressed close, but they were soft and devoid of spine or thorn. Water gushed from one side and they found a narrow brook flanked by mossy banks. Clusters of some grape-like fruit hung thickly from low branches and Dumarest gathered them, sitting, eating with quiet deliberation.

Mayenne said, "We aren't going to be able to leave here, are we?"

"We don't know that."

"I feel it." She sat close beside him, the bronze of her hair pressed against his cheek. "So much to happen so fast," she murmured. "A few days ago and my life seemed arranged. Nothing but work and travel and a slow fading as my skill died. Do you know what happens to old Ghenkas? They move lower and lower down the social scale. A few open schools of elocution. Some manage to find themselves a husband, but men are few who would be willing to tie their lives to entertainers of such reputation. Most kill themselves. Did you know that, Earl?"

Eating, he shook his head.

"You find that strange? But then you wouldn't know what it means to watch a part of yourself die. The voice loses flexibility, cracks, holds broken tones. To a Ghenka that is death. It is better to leave with a little pride. Each of us carries a gem which, when sucked, will yield poison. There is no pain."

"You have no way of knowing that," he said quietly. "But you are not going to die."

"By the gem, no. I had thought about it, but then I met you and—" She broke off, drawing a deep breath. "I love you, Earl. My life began when I met you. Still I cannot believe that you love me in return."

"Why do you find that strange?"

"I am a Ghenka."

"You are a woman who can sing like an angel," he corrected. "And you have given me happiness."

"As others have done?"

She reached up and touched him as he made no answer, letting her fingers trail across his cheek, the hard line of his jaw.

"As others have done," she said, and this time it wasn't a question. "But they lost and I have won—for now."

The brook made a little rippling sound and he wondered where the water came from and where it went. From the wall of the cliff, he assumed, manufactured from the rock itself, vanishing beyond the protecting force fields which must seal the valley. He finished the last of the fruit and washed his hands, ducking his head deep into the stream. The water was cold, filled with tiny bubbles, tasting of iron.

"Earl!" She lay on the bank, arms lifted, eyes expressive. "Earl!"

"You should eat something."

"I am hungry," she admitted. "But not for food. Must I starve?"

He held her close and felt the tiny tremors which ran beneath her skin. A creature afraid and needing reassurance. She saw the bleakness of his face.

"Is something wrong?"

"No."

"Do you feel that we are being watched?" Her laugh was a low caress. "My darling, does it matter if we are?"

He was not thinking of that. Tormyle had taken Gorlyk as a specimen to be examined, but Gorlyk was a male. To be thorough, a female would have to be examined also. Mari, Lolis or Mayenne. Which would be chosen?

She cried out from the pressure of his arms.

The sky never changed. Always it seemed as if it were noon, and Dumarest could only guess how long they had been away. Mayenne walked beside him, eating fruits he had gathered, golden juice on her lips and cheeks.

"You're a strange man, Earl. Here we are with all this trouble and yet you insist that I eat."

"An empty stomach doesn't help clear thinking," he said absently.

"But to worry about details when we've such a big problem. Aren't you concerned about the future?"

The future was to come; the present was at hand. Life was the extension of a moment and he had learned the lesson too well for it ever to be forgotten.

The group at the base of the ship seemed the same as before. Dumarest could see Chom's squat bulk, the more graceful shape of Daroca, Karn's open blouse, the two Qualish brothers, Mari.

"Earl!" Mayenne caught his arm. "Lolis isn't with them."

Lolis, young and fair and full of grace. Nubile and eager for love, a little foolish perhaps, more than a little selfish. Why had she been chosen?

"She went shortly after you'd left," said Karn dully. "Vanished just like Gorlyk. One second she was sitting there, making a garland out of some flowers, and then she was gone. Damn the thing!" he exploded. "Does it intend to kill us all?"

"It's playing with us," said Harg. "Like a cat with a mouse." His hands trembled as he dealt out cards. "One after the other. First Gorlyk, then Lolis; who next? Mari, perhaps? Chom? Me?" He grunted as he turned over the jester. "The fool," he said. "We're all fools. Why didn't we stay safely at home?"

"I've checked the ship," said Karn to Dumarest. "I tried to get inside. There are lasers there, weapons we could use if we had to. But it's still sealed tight."

"Weapons won't help us." Chom had overheard. "We need to use more subtle ways. The thing must be intrigued, bribed, seduced into letting us go free. A bargain must be made."

"We've been over this," said Karn. "We have nothing to offer."

"I disagree." Daroca brushed a fleck of pollen from his sleeve. "We know the thing is bored. We know that it needs something to hold its interest. A problem, perhaps. A paradox of some kind. There is one about a barber; do you know it?"

"There is a village in which all men are shaved by the barber," said Harg. "No man shaves himself. Question, who shaves the barber? Incidentally, every man in the village is clean-shaven."

"Stupidity!" snorted Mari. "Do you think Tormyle would be interested in a riddle like that?"

"He might be," said Daroca. "There is no answer, you understand. If all men are clean-shaven, and no man shaves himself, and all are shaved by the barber, then the barber cannot be shaved. But he is clean-shaven. Can you grasp the paradox?"

Mari said, "If our lives depend on a thing like that, then we had best end them now. Earl, can't you think of something?"

"Daroca could have a point," he said. "It's worth considering. It would do no harm to give it something to think about. Who knows? We may be lucky."

A voice said, "What is luck?"

It came from the base of the vessel and they turned, staring. Mari gave a choking noise and Chom sucked in his breath.

"God!" said Karn. "What is that?"

"I am Tormyle." The thing lurched forward. "What is luck?"

It was grotesque, a child's fantasy of an ogre, something which should have been a man but wasn't. It was tall and broad and the face held certain disturbing familiarities. Gorlyk, distorted, could have looked like that. Gorlyk, swollen, stretched, partly melted and then frozen into a parody of a human shape.

Again it said, "I am Tormyle. What is luck?"

Harg licked dry lips. "The combination of fortuitous circumstances. Why—"

"Why do I appear before you in this guise?" The voice was not as cold as before. It almost held interest. "To be viable in any frame of reference communication must be of an equal nature. It occurred to me that perhaps my previous method may have disturbed you. I learned much from the original specimen."

Dumarest said, "And the second one? The girl?"

"She is of a more complex character. My investigation is proceeding."

"You've killed them," said Mari bitterly. "You've torn them apart."

78 *E. C. Tubb*

"Destruction was essential for the complete reduction to elemental parts. But it is of no importance. The sample was small and can be replaced by your normal reproductive methods. Tell me about luck." It nodded as Harg explained. "I understand. The selection of variable choices so as to arrive at a desired result. To you it is important?"

"Yes," said the gambler.

A hand lifted, pointed. "You?"

"We had bad luck," said Mari. "That's why we're here."

"So the acquisition of luck is a prime directive?"

"Yes," said Harg.

"No," said Mayenne.

"Explain."

"A person has a certain thing which is of major importance in his life," she said. "Harg is a gambler and so he wants good luck. To me that isn't so important."

"What is?"

"Love."

"Love?" Tormyle sounded puzzled. "The word is familiar. The second specimen was obsessed with the concept. Love is what you did beside the stream?"

"That is part of it, yes."

"There is more? Yes. An intangible. An emotion. Data is accumulating. A correct decision to attempt communication by this method. More prime directives." The hand lifted. "You?"

Karn said, "I want command. Responsibility."

"You?"

Chom said, "To live in comfort."

"You?"

Dumarest said, "To survive."

"The basic prime function of any sentient being." Tormyle sounded approving. "A policy is being formulated to achieve the desired result. Later you will be notified. There will be darkness. You will rest."

It vanished.

The sky went dark.

They slept.

Chapter
◆ EIGHT ◆

Chom rose, muttering, his face creased as he stretched. "I ache," he complained. "At least Tormyle could have given us softer beds."

Dumarest glanced at the sky. It was bright again, shimmering. He felt stiff and unrested. They had lain where the thing had left them, falling into immediate unconsciousness when the sky had darkened. A forced period of sleep which had contained little of value.

Around him the others had risen. Daroca dusted down his clothing, the great ring on his finger flashing with reflected light.

"What have we learned?" he demanded. "It came to us and spoke; have we learned anything new?"

"A policy is being formulated," said Harg. "Something to achieve the desired result. What result?"

"The alleviation of its boredom," said Chom. He winced as he rubbed his back. "And we have nothing to offer it. Nothing."

Karn came from the vessel where he had been testing the port. "Still sealed. Earl, what should we do?"

He was the captain and should have made the decisions, but he was used to space and the obedience of machines. In this environment he was at a loss.

"We must get organized," said Dumarest. "We need food, shelter, beds, weapons."

"Weapons?"

It would give them something to do and, armed, they would feel less helpless.

"We don't know what Tormyle intends," explained Dumarest. "It is only good sense that we should prepare for anything we can imagine. We need beds so that we can rest in comfort. Food to maintain our strength. Shelter in case the environment is changed. But most important of all is that we remain active."

"Why?" demanded Chom. "We are helpless. Must we run like a rat in a wheel for the sake of movement?"

Daroca said, thoughtfully, "The analogy is a good one. When I was a boy I kept some insects in a jar. They were clever things and they amused me with their constructions. At times I used to tear down what they had built in order to watch them build again. After a time they ceased to spin their fabrications, and so, bored, I destroyed them. Earl is right."

"We are not insects."

"We are men," said Dumarest harshly. "No matter what Tormyle thinks of us, we are men. The moment we forget that we deserve to die."

"The man of action," said Chom. "But there is more to life than physical endeavor. There is the logic of the mind."

"Logic?" Daroca shrugged. "All men must die, and so it would be logical to anticipate the inevitable. Do you suggest we all terminate our existence?"

The entrepreneur scowled.

"You twist my words," he complained. "If we could think of something to intrigue Tormyle we could be gone in an hour. I still say we should concentrate on that."

Karn made his decision. "We'll do as Earl says."

There were difficulties. The gathering of ferns for the beds was simple, but they had to make baskets in which to hold the fruit, and Karn frowned as Dumarest mentioned water.

"We'll need pots. There could be clay in the soil, perhaps, but how can we harden it?"

"With fire." Dumarest sighed as he recognized the other's limitations. "Daroca has traveled and must have experience of nonmechanical cultures. And the Qualish brothers should know something of primitive engineering skills. A fire can be made with a bow to generate friction. Baskets can be woven from leaves; some of these plants could contain gummy saps which would make them water-tight. There are big leaves which could be sewn with a needle of wood and thread of fiber."

"And the material for spears? We need long branches. You have a knife, Earl. Will you gather them?"

A clump of slender boles reared to one side, slim, topped with feathery tufts, each twice the height of a man. Dumarest cut one down close to the ground and examined it. The material was hollow, like a tube, but one end could be sliced at an angle so as to make a point. He chopped it to an eight-foot length, poised it and threw it toward Karn. It stuck, quivering, in the soil.

"Will they do, Earl?"

"Try it."

The Qualish brothers came toward them as Karn threw the crude weapon.

Sac lifted it and flexed it in his hands. "Highly elastic," he commented as it snapped back into its former shape. "We could make bows out of this. All we need are some feathers for the arrows."

"Leaves would do," said his brother. He took the shaft and flexed it in turn. "Anything will serve for use as a flight. Our problem is in finding something suitable to use as a string." He plucked at his clothing. "Maybe we could tease out a few threads and wind them together. It's worth a try."

"Cut some more, Earl," said Karn. It had been a comfort to hold the spear. "As many as are suitable."

Dumarest returned to the clump. The knife in his hand flashed as it sheared through the slender boles, the feathery tips rustling as they fell. He reached for one to slice off the end and froze.

Tormyle stood before them.

It had changed. Now it no longer looked grotesque, but massively human. The rounded skull rose seven feet above the splayed feet. The neck was thick, running into sloping shoulders, the arms and chest corded with muscle. The face was a graven image and slanted eyes glowed from beneath prominent brows.

It said, "The original specimen considered this to be an optimum form. You agree? No. Some have reservations. I find it intriguing that there is no accepted norm for the shape of individuals of your species. However, it will serve for the matter at hand. I intend to test your prime directive. Certain limitations have been imposed for the purpose of this experiment."

"I don't understand," said Karn. "What do you mean?"

"The prime directive of any sentient life-form is to survive." A thick arm lifted and pointed at Dumarest. "You stated that on the previous occasion. Correct?"

"Yes," said Dumarest.

"You have repeated that conviction since wakening. In you it is very strong. In others not so strong. I am intrigued by the differential. Explain."

"All men want to live. Some are more eager for life than others."

"A variation of intensity. I understand. The strongest, then, should be tested. Failure will result in complete termination."

"My God!" whispered Karn. "Earl, it intends to fight you."

Dumarest backed as it advanced, knife poised in his hand, sword-fashion, edge upward so as to slash. To thrust would be useless; the corded muscle would be tough and even if penetrated would trap the blade. And he had no certainty that the thing held familiar organs. It was shaped like a man and there should be a heart, lungs and a brain. But how could he kill a planetary intelligence?

Tormyle said, "This body is fashioned after your own. The destruction of certain areas will cause it to cease functioning. Remember that you are representative of your species. Begin."

Dumarest threw himself to one side as it ran toward him. The knife blurred, hit and dragged as he drew it back in a vicious slash. Red fluid like blood gushed from Tormyle's side. A man would have clapped a hand to the wound, hesitated and perhaps withdrawn so as to resume the attack with more caution. Tormyle did not react like a man. Before Dumarest could recover his stance the thing was on him.

A blow jarred the side of his head and he tasted blood as he went down. A foot slammed into his ribs, lifted and stamped down at his face. It missed as he rolled and sprang to his feet. Again the knife lashed at the corded muscle and a long cut opened across the belly. Intestines should have bulged, bursting free to hang in red and blue ribbons; instead the wound gaped like a cut made in clay.

Tormyle moved back.

"We recommence," it said. "You have unnatural advantage. For the purpose of this test we must be even. The implement in your hand must be discarded."

Dumarest snarled and threw the knife.

It halted an inch before one of the deep-set eyes, hovered a moment, then spun through the air to land with a thud an inch from Karn's foot. Before it had landed, Dumarest had attacked. He ran forward, dropping, his right boot swinging in a vicious arc to the thing's left knee. It hit with the dull snap of bone. As a hand snatched at him he had rolled clear. Immediately he sprang to one side and kicked again, this time at the other knee. Crippled, the thing fell.

"Interesting application of mechanical principles," it said. "However, compensations can be made."

On its knees it shambled forward, hands outstretched.

Dumarest hesitated, glancing at the knife. If he ran for it, Tormyle would recommence the contest and he would have neither the blade nor the advantage he had won. An advantage gained only because the thing was unused to physical combat and lacked the hard-won experience Dumarest possessed.

But it could learn. Already it was moving faster, the big hands reaching out to rip and tear. To stop it bare-handed might be impossible, but it had to be tried.

Dumarest ran forward, jumped and landed just behind the broad back. He lifted his hand, stiffened the edge and swung it like an ax at the base of the neck. Again, a third time, then Tormyle had turned and the big hands gripped his thigh.

Dumarest stabbed it in the eyes.

"Ocular vision now destroyed," said Tormyle. "Severe damage to upper region of torso and lower region of guidance mechanism." It gurgled as Dumarest chopped it in the throat and then, quickly, slammed the edges of his palms at the biceps and nerves which would control the hands if the thing had been a man.

The grip of the fingers slackened. Dumarest pulled free, lifted his doubled fists and brought them crashing down on the thing's temple. Bone yielded beneath the sledgehammer impact. Again and the weakened skull showed a noticeable impression.

"Extensive damage to frontal lobes of directive unit," said Tormyle. "Had this fabrication been a sentient organism it would now be incapable of function. The test is over."

It vanished.

Between the mossy banks the stream made a liquid susurration, the surface flecked and dancing with light from the glowing sky above. Dumarest stripped and dived, hitting the water with a shower of spray, arching his back and arms so as to glide just beneath the surface. The water was as cold as before, numbing with its impact and he rose, gasping, ducking to scoop up a handful of fine grit from the bed. Standing in the water he rubbed the grime and stains from his hands. More grit and he cleaned his clothing; then he spread out his tunic and pants to dry. His thigh showed ugly bruises where Tormyle had gripped the flesh and his hands were sore and swollen. Lying on the bank, he let them trail in the water, the cold numbing and reducing the tenderness.

It was warm and the sultry air held the scent of growing things. Against the cliff the bulk of the ship reared, tall, incongruous in the valley paradise, and thinly he could hear the sound of voices. One of the Qualish brothers calling to the other, and the answer, Mari's higher voice, all muffled by the screen of vegetation. He turned at the sound of movement, a lilting thread of song.

"Mayenne?"

The song died and was replaced by a soft laugh. The rustle of disturbed leaves came closer.

"Is that you, Mayenne?"

He frowned as there was no answer and rose, stepping to where his knife stood half buried in the soil. Before he could reach it, she stepped from the undergrowth and stood smiling before him.

"Lolis! But—"

"Are you disappointed, Earl? Did you expect Mayenne?" She smiled and came closer. "What can she give you that I cannot? Earl, my darling, must you be so blind?"

She looked as he remembered, tall and young and very beautiful. She wore a thin gown of some diaphanous material which clung to the curves of her body. It parted as she sat to reveal the long lines of her thighs, the upper swell of her breasts. One hand patted the ground at her side.

"Come, Earl, sit and talk to me. Why do you look so surprised?"

He said harshly, "I thought you were dead. We all thought that."

"Dead, Earl?" Her laughter was as sweet as the tinkle of the water. "Do I look as if I am dead? I am here before you. Let us make love."

He ignored the invitation, sitting close beside her, his eyes probing her own. There was something beneath the surface, a touch of hardness he had never noticed before, an assurance she had previously lacked.

Quietly he said, "What is your name, my lady?"

"Lolis Egas. I was to have been married to Alora Motril of the House of Ayette."

"Was to have been?"

"I think that I have changed my mind. He no longer appeals to me. Come, Earl, let us make love."

"On the journey here, in the ship, there was a man who took you to see a beast. His name?"

"Really, Earl, does that matter?"

"His name?"

She did not hesitate. "Bitola."

"And your guard? You remember her name also?"

"Certainly. Hera Phollen. What is the matter, Earl? Why do you ask so many questions? Don't you trust me?"

For answer he reached out and took her wrist between his fingers. The flesh was smooth, warm and silken to his touch. He gripped and watched as the indentations he had made filled to leave small pink patches against the whiteness of her skin.

Flatly he said, "Lolis is dead. Both specimens were tested to destruction. Why did you select this shape, Tormyle?"

"You guessed," she said. "How?"

"Lolis was young and beautiful, but she would never have acted as calmly as you have done. You may have stored every fact you discovered in her mind, but her emotional interplay eluded you. What do you intend?"

"At the moment, nothing."

"And later?"

"That I have yet to decide." She leaned back on the mossy bank, turning so as to face him, smiling as if she were exactly what she appeared to be. "I like this form so much better than the other, don't you, Earl? And it allows for free communication. I decided that it would be best to appear in a shape familiar to you all. The other tended to create disturbing aberrations. A facet of the thing you call emotion. What would you call it? Fear. What is fear?"

"The anticipation of personal hurt or destruction."

"But you were not afraid when we fought, Earl. Why was that? Can't you experience the emotion?"

"Yes," said Dumarest bleakly. "I know what it is to be afraid. But fear has no place in combat. A man afraid is a man as good as dead. He slows, hesitates, misses his chances. When you are fighting for your life you have room for only one thought. To survive. Nothing else matters."

"Not even love?"

"Lolis would have put that first," he admitted. "But the girl was a romantic who had yet to learn the essentials of living."

"You miss her, Earl?"

"No."

"Could you have loved her?"

"How can I answer that?" He was impatient. "You have no idea as to the meaning of the word. What is love? Who can answer? Love takes many forms. To some it is a weakness, to others a source of strength. A man can love many things, his wealth, his life, his home, his children, his wife, his mother, his sisters and brothers, but each love is different from the rest." He added, "And some men never love at all."

"Are you one of them, Earl?"

"No."

"You have loved," she said softly. "And a man like you would love deep and well. You could tell me about it and teach me what it is. The girl thought she knew what love was, but now I see that it was a love of self. A facet of the prime directive of survival. For you love has a different meaning. I must discover what it is."

He said, "You could call it the converse of being cruel."

"Cruel?"

"You are being cruel in keeping us here. Why don't you repair the ship and let us go?"

"Later, perhaps."

"Can you do it? Repair the ship, I mean?"

"That?" Her laugh was pure merriment. "That has already been done. A simple matter of selected forces and synthesis of the missing parts. Your vessel is very elementary, Earl. I could build you a better one."

"That won't be necessary. Now, if you will unseal the ship, we'll be on our way."

He was being optimistic and he knew it, but it was worth a try. He was not disappointed when the girl shook her head.

"No, Earl, not yet. There are still things I have yet to learn. A' ''' 'uck, for example. The selection of fortuitous circumstances." She paused as if listening. "At this moment Harg is selecting a fruit from a tree. It is one of a cluster, and half of them are filled with a substance destructive to his metabolism. If his luck is good he will choose one which is harmless. Correct?"

Dumarest looked at his hands; they were clenched, the knuckles white. For a moment he was tempted to grab the girl by the throat and strangle her to death. But it would only be a temporary thing, and Harg could still select wrongly.

She said again, "Correct?"

"Yes."

"And if he picks one which is lethal, his luck would have been bad. Is that so?"

"Yes," said Dumarest again.

"He has chosen," she said after a moment. "And his luck was good. Now what made him pick that fruit and not one of the others? How often could he do it? What factor determined his selection?"

"An intriguing question," said Dumarest. "And one which has engrossed some of our finest thinkers for millennia. As yet they have found no answer. Perhaps you could."

"I will consider it."

"And, in the meantime, will you see that the fruits and everything else are harmless? If not, you will lose your specimens."

She smiled, teeth white against the redness of her lips, her throat. "You are concerned. Do you love them all so much?"

"That has nothing to do with it."

"What then?"

"I'm a specimen too," reminded Dumarest. "And my luck needn't be as good as Harg's."

"But concern is a part of love?"

"Yes."

"And what else? Sacrifice?" She rose before he could answer and waited until he stood before her. "A most intriguing concept and one which I must fully investigate. I will devise a plan. In the meantime there will be no further random experiments. The fruits and all else in the valley will be harmless as before."

"And the ship? When can we leave?"

For a moment she looked a young and lovely girl pondering on which dress to wear for a special occasion, and then he saw her eyes, the cold detachment, and remembered who and what she was. Remembered too that she could destroy them all at a whim.

"When I have discovered what love is," she said. "Not before."

Chapter
◆ NINE ◆

Chom lifted the bow, drew back the string and let fly. He swore as the arrow thudded into the dirt a good ten feet to one side of the tree they were using as a target.

Daroca said, "You plucked. Don't jerk the string back as you release. Just straighten the fingers when you're ready. See?" He demonstrated, the arrow hitting the bole. "Try again."

"What's the use?" Chom scowled as he rubbed his left arm. "I can't hit anything and the damn string's flaying my arm. I'll stick to a club."

"It's a matter of practice," insisted Daroca. "You have to keep trying. Wrap something around your arm to give protection. Pull the notched arrow back to the point of the chin and use the barb as a foresight. Look at what you are aiming at and release without plucking."

"I'll still stick to a club," said Chom firmly. "You learned how to use a bow when you were a boy; I didn't. I had no time for games. Anyway, what good is a thing like that against Tormyle?"

Harg said, "We won't be fighting Tormyle; not exactly. We could be up against something like Earl fought. Man-shapes or animal-forms of some kind. All we know is that we are to be tested in some way and have to be ready to meet anything that comes."

Chom made no further objection. Instead, he squatted and recommenced work on his club. A large stone had been wedged in the split end of a thick branch and lashed tight with strips of material pilfered from his blouse. Now he tied more strips so as to make a loop which could be slipped over the wrist.

To one side Dumarest was making knives.

He sat before a heap of the thin boles he had cut and sliced them at an angle. The edges of the hollow stems made sharp edges and a wicked point. He left the round handles untouched.

Mayenne said, "Will they be any good, Earl?"

"These?" He lifted one of the crude knives. "They can cut and thrust and will kill as surely as a blade of tempered steel. All we need to do is to wrap some thread around the hilts so as to stop the hand slipping along the edges."

She hadn't meant that and he knew it, but had deliberately misunderstood. As he reached for another foot of stem, she caught his hand.

"You were a long time at the river, Earl. I tried to join you, but there was a barrier of some kind which prevented me. What did it look like?"

"Tormyle? I told you. Like Lolis."

"She was very beautiful."

"So?"

"And you were bathing and naked and—" She broke off. "I'm sorry, Earl. I guess I'm just jealous. But when I think of you and her in the same place where we found happiness, well . . . forgive me?"

"For being in love?"

"For being a stupid fool. What does one woman more or less matter? And she isn't a woman, not really. Did you?"

"No."

"Would you have?"

He was coldly deliberate. "If it would have bought our freedom, yes. But it wouldn't and I didn't."

"I'm glad, Earl."

He smiled and stroked the edge of his knife down the length of wood. It was not as sharp as normal and he reached for a stone to whet the blade. Over the thin rasping Mayenne said, "When, Earl? Did it say?"

"No."

"Nor what we could expect?"

"I told you what she said. When she knows what love is, then she will let us go. Not before."

"She?"

"It, then. Tormyle. What difference does it make?" Cautiously he tested the whetted edge. "Try handling one of these knives. Get used to the feel and heft. Practice sticking one into the ground. When you do hold your thumb over the end and aim for a point about three inches below the surface." He frowned as she made no move to obey. "Do it, girl. Your life could depend on it."

Mari called out as Mayenne picked up one of the wooden slivers.

"Teach your woman to use a knife and you buy trouble, Earl. Haven't you learned anything in life?"

"To dodge," he said, matching her humor. "To fight when I can't and run when I can. Have you made that sling yet?"

"All finished." She held up a thonged pouch. "Can you really use one of these?"

For answer he slipped the knife into his boot, rose and took the sling from her hand. A pebble the size of an egg rested in the dirt. He picked it up, fitted it into the pouch and, holding both thongs, swung the sling about his head.

"That tree," he said. "The cluster of fruit."

The sling spun faster, whirring through the air, the stone hurtling as he released one of the thongs. Juice and pulp spattered the bole where the fruit had hung, the sound of the stone a soggy thud.

"I used to hunt with one when a boy," he said. "Game was small, scarce and agile. A sling was all I could afford."

"Not even a bow and arrows?"

"They were Daroca's idea. The Qualish brothers made them."

"And you don't think they'll be of much use?"

"Daroca can use one, but that's all. It takes a lot of practice to hit what you aim at with a bow. A crossbow would be different, but we can't make them with what's at hand."

Not if they were to have any stopping power, he thought. For that they needed a strong prod, heavy bolts and cord they didn't possess. And a heavy crossbow was troublesome to load. At close quarters a spear was as good. Closer and a club was better.

Karn came from the base of the ship, the Qualish

brothers at his side. The officer looked tired and haggard, his eyes revealing his frustration. Logic told him it would do little good to gain entry into the vessel, but to him it was home and he wanted to be in the familiar surroundings of his command.

"Nothing," he said to Dumarest's unspoken question. "We tried to force an entry through the emergency hatch. The whole ship's sealed solid. Are you sure it has been repaired?"

"So I was told."

"It could be a lie." Karn scrubbed at his chin. "But what would be the point in that? If only I could make certain."

"We'll try again," said Sac Qualish. "Later."

His brother said, "Should we build more weapons, Earl? We could make a catapult of some kind. Or construct an earthwork of sorts. A ditch and sharpened stakes in a ring around the ship."

"No," said Dumarest.

"You don't think it'll be necessary?"

"There's no point in tiring ourselves out making something we may not need. I don't know when this test is going to begin, but we want to be fresh to meet it. You'd better get some food and rest now. You too, Karn. There's not much more we can do but wait."

Wait and hope and practice and try to find the answer to a question. What was love?

And how to explain it to an alien intelligence who had no conception of the meaning of the word?

They had built a fire, a small thing of weak flames and a thread of coiling smoke which rose like a feather in the still air. Mari threw on a handful of dried leaves and set others to bake, coughing a little as the fumes caught her throat. Chom held a fruit speared on a thin wand and roasted it. He lifted the dripping mess, tasted it and spat his disgust.

"Fruit," he said. "Well, I suppose we could make wine if we had to, but I would give it all for a bite of decent meat."

Karn muttered in his sleep. "Seleem," he murmured. "Yes, sir. Full cargo on Ayette. Three riding Low."

Mayenne began to sing.

It began as a low dirge, tremulous, haunting, a bleak call for help from the midst of snowy wastes and endless deserts, the empty expanse of enormous seas and the barren vault of the skies. It rose a little, a thread of pure sound in which lurked words like ghosts, fragments of half heard, half understood communication, touching buried memories so that the past lived again. Gath and the endless winds, the fretted mountains, the medley of voices, the composite of all the sounds that had ever been or could ever be made. A voice whispering.

"I love you, Earl. I love you!"

Another.

"A thousand years of subjective sleep. A milliard of dreams."

A third.

"There will always be a welcome for you on Toy . . . on Jest . . . on Hive . . . on Technos . . . on Dradea."

More.

"No, Earl! No! . . . ten High passages . . . the Ram, the Bull, the Heavenly Twins . . . five hundred, ten-inch knives, to the death . . . I love you, Earl. I love you!"

And another, utterly cold, speaking across the galaxy with frigid determination.

"Find him at all costs. Failure will not be tolerated. The man Dumarest has the secret the Cyclan must repossess. Find him!"

A bell chiming.

"Charity, brother. Remember the credo of the Church. There, but for the grace of God, go I. Charity . . . charity . . . charity."

The song wavered a little, soared almost to a scream, then plunged into a throbbing undertone reminiscent of drums.

Daroca sighed. "Artistry," he murmured. "Never have I heard a Ghenka sing so well."

"If I can remain alive," said Chom with feeling, "and if I can gather the needed wealth, I shall buy a Ghenka for my private pleasure."

"A recording would be cheaper," said Harg.

"True, but would it be the same? I think not. No true artist sings exactly the same twice; each performance is unique to itself. And the mood is important—how could any recording guess my thoughts, the way I feel, the adaptions essential to the creation of the moment? No, my friend, I have made my decision." He speared another fruit and held it over the flames. "Perhaps this one," he murmured. "At least it may not dissolve into a pulp."

Mari said, "Earl, look at the ship. Something is happening."

A light glowed around the supports, a will-o'-the-wisp luminescence bright even against the glare of the sky. It gathered itself into a ball and drifted toward them. It touched the ground a few feet away. Touched—and changed.

An insect, thought Dumarest wildly. Standing upright, winged, haloed with light, the face a mask of perfection.

"An angel," whispered Mari. "Dear God, an angel!"

A figment of some old religion caught and fashioned from the aroused images of her mind. A fragment of legend brought to solidity by the magic of Tormyle. For a moment it stood resplendent and then it was gone and in its place stood a familiar shape.

"Lolis!" Chom's fruit fell unheeded into the fire. "My lady!" He rose, bowing, his hands outspread. "I know, of course, that you are not the person we knew by that name. But it will serve. A lovely name for a lovely woman. My lady, I understand that you wish to know the meaning of love. I can teach you. In my travels I have come against it in many forms and have mastered them all. My heart is yours to command."

She said, "The shape I wore before did not please you. It should have. Why didn't it?"

"I am a simple man, my lady, and used to simple ways. Not for me the esoterics of mysterious cults. I buy and I sell and do what I can to please. Love, to me, is the desire to serve. To serve, to teach, to guide. To give pleasure and, if in return I gain a little joy, it is the joy of giving. If I could talk to you, my lady, alone, I am sure that we could find matters of mutual interest."

Mari said, "I don't trust that man. He's trying to make a private deal. Doesn't the fool realize that he's not talking to a normal woman?"

She had spoken softly but her voice had carried. Daroca

glanced at Dumarest, then at Karn. The officer cleared his throat.

"As acting captain I represent these people. Any arrangements should be made through me."

"Captain?"

"I am in command of the vessel." Karn was bleary-eyed, freshly woken and unrested by his tormented sleep. He made a vague gesture toward the ship. "Tell me the price for letting us go."

The girl smiled, young and lovely and as fresh as a spring morning. She moved a little closer to where the fire plumed its thread of smoke. To one side Mayenne slammed her wooden knife viciously into the ground.

"We know the price," she snapped. "The thing wants the answer to a question. It wants to know what love is. Love!" she repeated bitterly. "How can you teach a planet what that is? How can you love a world?"

"It's possible," said Daroca softly. "If the world is home."

Earth, perhaps; but it wasn't the same and Dumarest knew it. Daroca was playing with words and this was no time for semantic games. It was no accident, he thought, that Tormyle had chosen to appear in a female guise. It could have copied Gorlyk's form as easily as that of Lolis. Why had it chosen to appear as a woman? He glanced to where Mayenne stabbed at the ground in symbolic murder. Had she reason for her jealousy?

Aloud he said, "We are not in the mood for games. You have made a decision; tell us what it is."

"Impatient, Earl?"

"We spoke once of cruelty. To keep people in suspense is not kind when their lives depend on your decision."

"And love is the converse of cruelty. I remember. And you, Earl, could never love a person who is cruel." She glanced at Chom. "Could you?"

"Love, my lady, knows no limitations. I could love you even while dying in your embrace."

She raised her arms and reached toward him and he moved toward her as if without a will of his own. His boots trod in the fire and scattered the ashes so that he became wreathed in smoke. In the smoke they embraced, his thick arms clasping the slender figure, her own arms around his plump torso, the hands pressing against his back.

"Love me," she said, and squeezed.

Chom made a sound like an animal in pain. His muscles bulged, the flesh of his cheeks mottling with a purple effusion of blood, his eyes starting from their sockets. Desperately he fought against the constriction and then, abruptly, relaxed, his face strained as he stared at the girl holding him close.

"Not the same," she said. "Not the same at all."

"My lady!" he wheezed. "My lady, please!"

She released him and he staggered back, tearing at the collar of his blouse.

"The problem is one of definition," she said. "To be genuine love must be strong, this much I have gathered. But love seems to hold many forms, and which is the right one? To discover this I have devised an experiment. It should be conclusive."

"Wait," said Harg. He stepped forward, a small man, aged, yet holding a strange dignity. "Listen to me, Lolis ... Tormyle, whoever you are. I don't understand all this talk of love. Maybe I've been unlucky in my time, but no woman has ever wanted me for her own and I've never felt strongly about anything. Certainly not strongly enough to fight and die for it. And I guess that is what you intend. So let's cut out all this nonsense and decide things one way or the other. A turn of a card. High card, you win and do with us as you please. Low card, and we win and you let us go. Quick, simple and decisive. You agree?"

"A gamble," she mused. "A test of the thing called luck. Do you all wish to participate?"

"Yes," said Dumarest quickly. "We do."

He caught Chom's arm as the man opened his mouth to protest and caught Daroca's look of sudden understanding. It was a wager they couldn't lose. Harg had framed the terms well; already they were in Tormyle's power to do with as it wished.

"Harg is in love with the laws of chance," she said. "For him joy lies in winning, and the touch of cards and dice are equal to a caress. Luck is his mistress and good fortune his deity. A strange thing," she mused, "that a sentient being could hold such high regard for something so intangible. But the concept is intriguing. Yet the wager is wrong. He stands to lose nothing."

Dumarest said, "You heard the terms. Do you agree?"

"To the gamble, yes. But not on those terms. Each must risk his own fortune. Harg will be first. If he wins, I will set him down on a safe place. If he loses, then I will take his life."

"A safe place," said Harg. "What do you mean?"

"A world on which you could survive. One of your habitated planets." She paused. "Ayette? Yes, the world you know as Ayette."

"You can do that?"

It was possible. To an entity which had snatched the ship across light-years in a second anything was possible. Harg had asked only for reassurance. When it came he produced his cards.

"Wait," said Dumarest sharply. "It's your life, man. Remember that."

"My life," said Harg. "Such as it is."

"Don't be a fool," said Mari harshly. "Go to the table expecting to lose and you'll be ruined for sure. As a gambler you know that. Stay with us and you've got a chance. Lose and you've got none at all." Her lips tightened as he riffled the deck. "Remember our agreement? Shares in a new house? Don't do it, Harg."

He ignored her, riffling the deck. He held them out on the flat of his palm.

"Choose."

"You first."

He cut quickly, trusting his life to the luck he had wooed over too many years. The cards made a slight rasping sound and he held his choice low, not looking at it, eyes instead on the young girl as she reached for the pack.

"A lady!" Sweat burst out on his forehead, clung like dew to his upper lip. His laugh was bitter as he turned up his own selection. "A jester! Well, I was always a fool. What now, Tormyle?"

He died.

He did it slowly, horribly, his flesh melting and seeming to run like wax in a flame. His limbs arched, became grotesque and his body puffed so that, as he fell, he looked like some monstrous spider. And, as he fell, he screamed.

Dumarest moved. He was a blur as he reached and snatched a spear, lifted it, thrust it with the full power of arms and shoulders into the shrieking mass. The sharpened point sliced deep, penetrated the heart and brought instant oblivion.

As Harg slumped into a lifeless heap he jerked free the spear and threw it at the smiling face of the girl.

The point, ugly with blood, dissolved into splinters, the shaft lifting to fall to one side.

Quietly she said, "That is twice you have used weapons against me, Earl. Will you never learn?"

"You bitch!" shouted Mari. "You dirty, sadistic bitch! Did you have to do that?"

"He wagered and he lost." And then, to Dumarest: "You killed him. For love?"

"For mercy—something you could never understand."

"Because he was in pain? Yet had you left him alone he would not have terminated his existence. I was altering his structure, adapting it to a new form. An experiment to discover how malleable your species is. Now, perhaps, I shall have to use another." Her arm lifted, pointed at Tek Qualish. "You."

He vanished.

To Mayenne. "You."

She followed.

To Mari and Karn. "You also."

They went and she followed.

Daroca had rebuilt the fire, gaining some small comfort from the flame, huddling close to it as his forebears had done in ancient times when the red glow had spelled safety and the communion of kind. Facing him, Sac Qualish sat with his head in his hands mourning his brother.

"A bad business," said Chom. He glanced uneasily over his shoulder to where Dumarest was busy selecting spears. Harg had gone, not even a patch of blood marring the ground where he had fallen. "A warning, perhaps? Harg tried to be clever, but he forgot that he was not dealing with a young and ignorant girl. How can any man hope to best the might of a planetary brain?"

"He tried," said Dumarest curtly.

"He tried and failed and died with your spear in his

heart. You were too quick, Earl. You should have waited. If the girl spoke the truth he could be alive now. Changed, but alive."

"As what?" Dumarest dropped two of the spears and hefted two others. "A thing to crawl in the dirt? A crippled freak?"

"He had a clean death," said Daroca. "No man could ask for more. If the same thing happens to me I hope that Earl will be as merciful." He shivered and held his hands close to the flame. "Is it my imagination or is it getting cold?"

Dumarest glanced up at the sky. It seemed lower than before and the upper regions of the ship shone with a sparkling frost. Around them the leaves seemed wilted, hanging limply from their stems. He walked toward the ship and felt the bite of numbing cold. Returning, he headed down the valley and felt the familiar heat. Back at the fire he said, "It's localized and spreading."

Chom was shrewd. "To keep us away from the vessel? But what's the point? It's sealed and we can't get in anyway."

"We'll find out," said Daroca. "When it's ready to let us know." He threw more leaves on the fire, added slivers of wood and leaned back from the rising smoke. "I've been thinking. We know that Tormyle is bored. We also know that it wants to discover the meaning of the emotion we know as love. But it is alien and that could well be impossible. What happens if it fails?"

"We die," said Chom bleakly.

"Perhaps not, at least, not in the way you mean. Time cannot mean the same to Tormyle as it does to us. I think that, while we continue to amuse it, we will continue to survive."

"Amuse?"

"Intrigue, then. Interest would be a better word. What do you think, Earl?"

"I think we should get armed," said Dumarest. "And be ready to move."

"To where?" Sac Qualish lifted his head. His face was strained, bitter, his eyes red. "To run in a circle until that thing takes us like it did my brother? To take us and tear us apart like it did Gorlyk and Lolis? To change us like it did Harg? Do you remember what he looked like? When I think of Tek like that it makes me want to vomit."

"Shut up," said Chom, and added, more gently: "Tek wasn't the only one. He took the Ghenka too, remember."

"And Mari and Karn," mused Daroca. "Now why should it have made that selection?"

"Does it matter?"

"It could," insisted Daroca. "The girl was, is, in love with Earl. Tek and his brother are very close, and brotherly love can be very strong. Karn? Well, he is in love with his ship."

"And Mari?" Chom blew out his cheeks and shook his head. "Once I thought that she might have a fancy for Harg, but he is dead now. You perhaps? Are you in love with her?"

"No, but her profession is to deal in love, or what too many people call it. It is her business and her thoughts must be conditioned to regard her houses as palaces of joy, mansions of endearment, abodes of love. We know the difference; but would Tormyle?"

"A professional dealer in the emotion it seeks to understand," said the entrepreneur slowly. "If our situation wasn't so perilous I would find the concept amusing."

But there was nothing amusing in the growing cold, the sealed ship, the too recent memory of the way Harg had died. And still less in the voice which whispered from the wilting leaves, the very air itself.

"The experiment begins. Those who were taken will be found at the end of the valley. Your actions will determine their continued existence. Go now."

"Tek alive!" Sac sprang to his feet, his eyes glowing. "Did you hear that? They're still alive!"

Alive and waiting to be rescued, the bait in an alien trap to determine an emotion impossible for their captor to comprehend.

Chapter
◆ TEN ◆

The valley had changed. The cold welling from the region of the ship had blighted the vegetation and turned the stream to ice, but it was more than that. Now every leaf held a hint of menace as if things watched from behind its cover and thin threads glistened with silver between the trees.

A maze, thought Dumarest, through which they were being guided, spurred by the advancing cold and urged by the bait lying ahead. Mayenne and the others. Thought of the Ghenka lengthened his stride. She would be waiting, hoping. He could not fail her.

Yet, even so, he was cautious.

"Wait," he snapped as Sac Qualish plunged ahead. "Take it easy. We don't know what may be waiting for us."

"My brother is waiting, that's all I care about."

"Can you help him if you're dead?" Dumarest halted and glanced around. The trees soared high, their feathered tops hiding the sky and casting patches of thick gloom. The ground felt soggy and he trod carefully down a narrow path. They had left the cold behind and, here, it was still warm.

Chom sucked in his breath as something moved to one side.

"What was that?"

A thing, a shape, something fashioned at Tormyle's whim. It appeared again, low, crouching, eyes like gems in an armored carapace. A watchdog, perhaps, to keep them on their way, or perhaps something to be feared more than that.

101

Dumarest said, "Daroca, your bow."

"You want me to kill it, Earl?"

"If you can." He watched as the other man took aim, drawing back the arrow, holding, then releasing the string with a vicious hum. The arrow whispered between the trees and hit with a hollow thud.

It was like bursting a balloon. There was an empty plop and a scatter of segments. Chom sighed his relief.

"If that's all we have to face we haven't much to worry about." He lifted his club and swung it against a tree. The stone made a dent in the soft bole. In his other hand he carried a spear and two of the wooden knives were thrust in a band tied around his waist. "We could stand off an army of the things."

"Perhaps," admitted Dumarest. "But not if we get separated. And there could be something else. Keep close and cover each other. You to one side, Chom; you the other, Sac; Daroca, take the rear." He paused and added, "And keep an arrow on the string, just in case."

He moved ahead, spear extended in both hands, ready to thrust or block. It was a clumsy thing compared to the quick mobility of the knife he was used to, but it had the advantage of length. Like the others, he carried wooden knives. Sac had a club. Daroca had his bow. Like savages, they plunged into the deepening gloom.

"What now?" Sac fumed his impatience as Dumarest halted again. "Damn it, Earl, we'll get nowhere like this. Why don't we just push on and find the others?"

"Through that?" Dumarest pointed with his spear. Ahead the path was crossed with silver threads.

"If we have to, yes." Sac pushed ahead. His spear touched one of the strands. The ground opened beneath it.

He yelled once as he fell and then Dumarest caught him by the arm, dropping the spear and flinging himself to the edge of the opening. Below gaped emptiness, a hollow void smoothed as if by machines. Sac hung, suspended, his spear falling like a splinter to vanish in darkness. His face, strained, turned upward to look at Dumarest.

"Earl! For God's sake!"

He was heavy and the ground at the edge of the hole loose. Dumarest gritted his teeth and concentrated on clamping his fingers about the arm, feeling the weight of the body tear at his muscles as the dirt below him fell into the hole. Then Chom had gripped his ankles, hauling back with all his weight. Sac rose, caught at Dumarest and heaved. One foot lifted to rest on the edge of the hole and, with a rush, he was safe, sweating as he rolled on the dirt.

"Trip wires," said Chom. "I don't understand this. If Tormyle wants us to reach the end of the valley, why does it make it so hard?"

"Perhaps it wants us to give up," suggested Daroca. "But then why the cold? We have no choice but to move. Rats in a maze," Daroca said thoughtfully. "I saw an experiment like that once. Food was placed at one end and the rats at the other. They wanted the food, but they had to move through the passages to get it. And there were dangers, things which drove them to frustrated madness, other things which killed. The idea was to find the most clever rat or the one with the greatest compulsion."

"We aren't rats," said Sac. He stood, trembling, looking at the hole. "You saved my life, Earl. I was falling, as good as dead, and you saved me. From now on you give the orders and I'll obey."

Dumarest looked at the silver wires, the shadowed path. To one side came the hint of movement; who could tell what lurked above?

He said, "We go back."

"To the ship?" Sac hesitated; he had made a promise which already he found hard to keep. "But what about the others? My brother?"

"We'll skirt the valley and keep the cliffs to one side. That way we'll only have to watch our flank."

"If we can get to the cliffs," said Daroca quietly. He lifted his bow and pointed with the arrow. More shapes had appeared, clustering, moving as if to a plan. They were difficult to spot and details were vague in the gloom, but they looked different from the one he had shot.

Chom drew in his breath.

"They're cutting us off," he said grimly. "Earl?"

"We charge. Together now and stop for nothing. Keep an eye open for wires and miss the trees. There is a clearing back a little way. Make for it and, if we have to, we'll make a stand. Now!"

He led the way, running, spear at the ready and eyes darting from side to side. A glint of silver showed ahead and he veered, the others following in his path. Another and he sprang aside, a third and he regained the trail he had left. Before him something rose from the ground, mandibles snapping, rearing half the height of a man. The spear caught it in the thorax, spilled a flood of ichor and ripped free as Dumarest jumped. His boot hit the flat head and the rounded back; then he was running to turn and stab fiercely at a worm-like thing which hissed and coiled and then vanished.

"Earl!" Chom came running, with Sac and Daroca following. "Behind you!"

He spun, dropping to one knee, the spear point sloping before him. A beast, striped and fanged, was in the air. The point sheared into chest and lungs, the slender shaft snapping beneath the weight. Dumarest dropped it, whipped out a wooden knife and plunged it into an eye.

"Quick!"

He was running again while behind him came the thrum of a bowstring, the soggy impact of Chom's club. Sac cried out, swearing, and pounded after the rest. Ahead lay the clearing, a patch of open ground coated with soft grass and edged by slender shafts. Dumarest raced toward them, the knife lifting from his boot, slashing, turning the hollow stems into fresh spears.

Panting, he looked around.

Nothing.

No nightmare beasts or shapes from delirium. No silver threads. No attack. Only himself and the others, gasping, hands strained as they gripped their weapons. And, as he watched, their breaths plumed in streams of vapor from the sudden cold.

"Madness," said Daroca. He stumbled and dragged himself upright with a visible effort. His face was lined, haggard, suddenly aged. Gone was the smooth dilettante who had ridden the ships down the odd byways of space for the sake of novelty. Now he, like them all, was a man struggling to survive.

"Madness," he said again. "What kind of test is this? What has it to do with the determination of love?"

Dumarest said nothing, plunging ahead, the soaring cliffs to his left, the massed vegetation to his right. As he had guessed the going was easier, a wide patch of debris lying between the cliff wall and the undergrowth, and though it was strewn with boulders they were making good time. Since they had left the clearing, they had seen no silver threads, no lurking shapes.

Only the numbing cold had followed them, forcing them to keep moving.

"We could make a fire," said Chom. "Sit and rest and maybe sleep a little. Food too; there must be fruit on some of those trees."

"We'd freeze," said Sac.

"Maybe not. If we showed determination, what would be the point in killing us?"

"We keep going," said Sac doggedly. "My brother is waiting."

"Then let him wait!" Chom slammed his club at a boulder, chips flying from beneath the impact. "What is your brother to me? If he's dead, there's no hurry; if he's alive, he can be patient. If we sit and refuse to move, she may come to us again. Words could accomplish more than this journey."

Dumarest said, "Remember Harg? What happened to him?"

"He gambled and lost."

"Do you want to take the same chance?"

The entrepreneur scowled. "No, but need it come to that? We have played her game long enough. If she wants love, there are four of us here to give it to her. No woman respects a man who acts like a mouse."

"She isn't a woman," said Dumarest. "Why don't you remember that?"

Dumarest realized it was easier for them to think of Tormyle in familiar terms: somehow a woman was less frightening than a totally alien being. But she was no more a woman than the shapes which had attacked them, the planet on which they trod. She, it, was all of them and more.

Daroca stumbled again, dropping his spear in order to catch a boulder and save himself. He clung to the stone, panting, sweat dewing his face despite the chill. Old, soft, he could no longer stand the pace.

"Leave me," he gasped. "I'll come after you as soon as I can."

Chom beat his hands together; his skin was mottled with the cold.

"He'll die," he said dispassionately. "If you are merciful, Earl, you will give him a fast end."

"Kill him?" Sac looked from one to the other. "You must be joking. You just can't kill a man like that."

"No?" Chom shrugged. "You have a weak stomach, my friend, and a selfish mind. The product of a soft world with neat laws and easy comforts. But I have lived on harsh planets and so has Earl. On such worlds a man must rely on his friends. What would you do with him? Carry him? We have far to go and are weak. Leave him? He will sit and freeze and shiver, then finally sink into a coma and die a miserable death. A thrust of a spear, a pressure on the carotids and it is over. Quick, clean, merciful."

"Barbaric!"

Sac was wrong, but Dumarest didn't argue. The man was a product of his culture and not to blame for the unconscious sadism which would condemn a man to lingering agony in the mistaken belief that he was being kind. But Chom was wrong also; the mercy of death was not a thing to be casually given to save inconvenience. Daroca was exhausted, ready to give up, but all men held within themselves unsuspected reserves of energy.

He said, "Daroca, listen to me."

"Leave me, Earl. Let me rest."

"If you stay here you'll die," said Dumarest harshly. "Is that what you want, to commit suicide? Now stand up, man. Up!" He gripped the blouse and pulled Daroca upright, away from the support of the boulder. Deliberately he sent the flat of his hand across the sunken cheek. Again, a third time, the blows measured to sting. He saw the shock in the sunken eyes, the dawning of anger. Rage was an anodyne to apathy and apathy could kill.

"Earl! Damn you!"

"You hate me," said Dumarest. "Good. And you hate this valley and Tormyle and what it is doing to us. You hate it so much that you aren't going to let it win. You're going to reach the end of the valley with the rest of us. All you have to do is to keep putting one foot before the other. A child could do it."

Daroca touched his cheek, the red marks left by Dumarest's fingers.

"No, Earl. I haven't the strength."

"I saw a woman once on Jachlet. She crawled ten miles with two broken legs. Haven't you the guts of that woman?" His hand lifted again, poised to strike. "Now move, damn you! Move!"

Sac took the lead, Daroca stumbling after him, leaning on his spear, the bow slung over his shoulder. Chom stayed close and Dumarest took the rear. Before them the cliff wall curved to the right, blending with the vegetation ahead. Above, the shimmering sky threw an even brightness. There was no sound, only the rasp of their boots, the sound of their breathing, the gasps of the exhausted man.

It was like a nightmare in which there was continuous movement but no progress. A false world of unreality in which anything could happen, the cliffs, the sky itself the product of a whim. The boulders grew larger, cracks appeared in the surface, and once the air became filled with drifting motes of sparkling dust.

Chom wiped at his sleeve and ran the tip of his tongue over his lips.

"Sweet," he said. "Like sugar."

Dumarest cautiously tasted it, gathered a small heap in the palm of his hand. It had a strong flavor and a texture like that of nuts. Food, perhaps, a gift from Tormyle? A reward for good behavior?

"Leave it," he said. "Don't eat it."

Chom frowned, "Poison?"

"No, but we have no water and it will aggravate our thirst."

They pressed on. The sparkling motes vanished as the valley stretched before them. Ahead thrust a jutting wall of rock, a barrier over which they had to climb. A crevasse had opened to their right which was impossible to cross.

"We could go back," said Chom. "Take a detour through the undergrowth."

Dumarest looked back the way they had come. The crevasse curved so as to enclose them in a narrow segment and, as he watched, it widened, moving close.

"We climb," he said. "We have no choice."

At first glance the wall was sheer, but then he saw minor imperfections, cracks, fretted and splintered stone, a ladder which an agile man could climb. Sac went ahead, Chom following, crawling up the face of the wall like an ungainly spider, thick shoulders heaving as he lifted his bulk.

Daroca said, "I can't make it, Earl. I haven't the strength."

"You'll make it."

"How? Can you give me skills I don't possess? I have no head for heights and I couldn't support my weight. You have no choice but to leave me."

Dumarest studied him. He was drawn, pale, haggard with fatigue. A man at the limit of his reserve. But he was slim, light and could be carried for a short distance. Carefully he studied the face of the wall. The others had reached halfway to the summit, scrabbling as they sought for holds. As he watched, Chom slipped, hung suspended by one arm and then, with a burst of energy, swung himself to safety.

But there was another route, one which offered more promise: a slanting crack running high across the wall, a ledge, a series of fretted places.

Daroca said, "You'd best hurry, Earl. The crevasse is very close."

It was feet away, moving as he watched, widening, the bottom invisible.

Dumarest threw aside his spear.

"Climb onto my back," he ordered. "Put your arms around my neck. Hold tight, but don't throttle me. Close your eyes if you have to, but relax. Don't fight against me."

"No, Earl. You can't do it."

"Move, damn you!"

The stone was granulated, sparkling with buried minerals, little gleams appearing to vanish inches before his eyes. Steadily he moved upward, balancing the weight on his back which threatened to tear him loose, muscles cracking as he gripped and hauled. He reached the slanting crack and moved along it, boots wedged tight to support his weight. In his ear the sound of Daroca's breath was a rasping susurration and he could feel the heat of the man, his sweat, his barely controlled fear.

"Relax," he said harshly.

"Earl!"

"I've climbed mountains before carrying a pack as heavy as you. We'll make it."

He reached the end of the slanting crack, groped upward for a fresh hold and felt rock crumble beneath his fingers. For a moment he swayed, fighting for balance; then his searching hand found a nub of stone, a rounded boss which he gripped as his boot rasped at the wall. It found a hold and he heaved upward, his other hand lifting.

"To the left," whispered Daroca. "A foot to the left and three inches upward."

Dumarest grunted. "Too far. Look for another higher but closer."

"Up," said Daroca. "More. To your right. There!"

It helped. Face close to the stone, Dumarest inched upward, guided by the whispering voice, using discarded handholds as resting places for his boots. He felt his muscles begin to weaken, the sting of sweat in his eyes and the taste of blood in his mouth as he clung desperately to the rock. The weight dragging at his back seemed to have increased and he knew that if he didn't make the summit soon he wouldn't make it at all.

Grimly he resisted the thought, concentrating on each movement as it came, not thinking of the inevitable result should he slip or lose his precarious balance. From somewhere above came the sound of voices and they spurred him on. If he could hear them they must be close.

"Earl!" Daroca's voice was a strained whisper. "I'm slipping. I can't hold on!"

"Lock your hands." He felt the sudden shift of balance, the backward tug. "Damn you! Do as I say!"

He choked as the locked fingers pressed against his throat, then tensed the muscles of his neck as he sucked in air. Another foot of upward progress, two more, and he paused, fighting the blackness which edged his vision.

Daroca's foot found a resting place and he heaved, easing the pressure of his hands.

"Earl, I—"

"Shut up. Look for holds. Tell me where they are."

Dumarest listened, memorizing, then inflated his lungs. With a smooth surge of energy he recommenced to climb, hands following a preconceived pattern, calling on the last of his strength. A yard, three, and then he felt hands grip his arms, pulling, dragging him and his burden to safety over the edge.

He rolled, feeling Daroca fall away, rising on all fours, head low as he sucked air into his tortured lungs. His arms were quivering, the muscles of back and shoulders, his calves and thighs. Above the surge of blood in his ears he heard Sac's voice, high, brittle with surprise.

"The valley! It's changed!"

Chapter

◆ ELEVEN ◆

There had been stone and a gentle slope leading from the edge of the cliff to a cluster of vegetation, trees thick with bushes filling the area to either side while, beyond, a curtain of mist had reared. The slope remained, some of the trees and a scatter of bushes, but where they had been thick now they were sparse, gathered in small copses interspersed with an emerald green sward. Where mist had curtained the end of the valley a thing of dreams now stood.

It rose in a mass of soaring towers, delicate spires and graceful cupolas, crenellated walls bright with streaming banners. A fortress such as had never existed in reality— the needs which had made such a thing imperative based in an age when its construction would have been impossible.

Dumarest examined it, eyes narrowed, catching the glint of metal against the somber stone. Helmets, perhaps, or the heads of spears, the glints vanished as soon as they were seen, flashing like will-o'-the-wisps, tiny flickers which teased the eyes.

Beside him Chom released his breath in a gusting sigh.

"Magic," he said. "Or madness. What game is the creature playing now?"

"A castle." Daroca rubbed at his red-rimmed eyes. "And are those soldiers on the walls?"

"It wasn't there before." Sac seemed dazed by what he had seen. "And then, as you came over the edge, Earl, it suddenly appeared. The mist seemed to solidify, the trees to blur and then—" His arm rose, making a helpless gesture.

"A castle," Daroca said again. "The concept of chivalry

111

and of romantic love. Has Tormyle locked the others within those walls? Are we supposed to rescue them? And, if so, how can the four of us storm that citadel?"

"We'll storm it," said Sac. "If we have to. My brother's in there. Right, Earl?"

"Four men," said Chom. "No weapons to speak of. You must be mad."

"Earl?"

"Shut up," said Dumarest. It was no time to quarrel. "We'll do what has to be done, but first let us find out what it is. Are you fit to move, Daroca?"

"With care, yes."

Dumarest nodded and led the way down the slope toward the enigmatic building. The ground was soft beneath his boots, the trees and bushes bright with clustered blooms, great floral stars of red and purple, globes of violet and azure, trailing fronds of scarlet and lambent green. An illustration from a child's storybook, he thought. Something stolen from a vagrant memory. Mari's perhaps, or even Karn's. Men who spent their lives in space had peculiar ideas as to recreation.

The slope flattened and then began to rise toward the castle. Details still remained vague; the walls were clear enough, the turrets and banners, but the hints of metallic gleaming defied true description. They could belong to the accouterments of men or things fashioned in the likeness of men. Or they could be the offshoot of opposed energies.

Chom came grumbling from where he had examined a clump of bushes. "No fruits. Nothing to eat or to assuage our thirst." He grimaced at the glowing sky. "And it seems to be getting warmer."

The heat increased as they progressed until the sweat was running down their faces. Dumarest eased his collar and tried not to think of rippling streams, the chill impact of crushed ice against his teeth. At his side Daroca stumbled and halted, panting.

"A moment," he pleaded. "If we could sit for a while and rest I'll be fit again. An hour, surely, can make little difference."

Sac forged ahead. "My brother is waiting. We have no time to rest."

His brother, Mayenne, the others. Yet exhausted men

would be of little use in what could be waiting ahead. Dumarest slowed, then headed toward a clump of trees. Shade, at least, was there to be enjoyed.

From the castle came the sound of a trumpet, hard, imperious.

It came again, a compelling note which seemed to hang in the crystalline air, urgent, summoning. A third time and Daroca sucked in his breath.

"The drawbridge," he whispered. "Look!"

It was a slab of wood, thirty feet high, ten broad. As they watched, it lowered, moving quickly, silent until it reached the ground, where it came to rest with a dull thud. Beyond it gaped an opening, dark, fretted at its upper edge with the teeth of a portcullis. Again the trumpet sounded and something came from the darkness toward them.

Like the castle, it was a thing of dreams: a tall figure mounted on a horse, both mount and rider plated with gleaming metal which shone like gold in the light from the sky. A lance rested in one gauntleted hand, the tip rising in salute as the thing came to a halt facing the little group. From within the closed helmet boomed a hollow voice.

"Welcome."

A herald, thought Dumarest. A part of the furnishings of this present fantasy, as was the castle, the drawbridge, the portcullis. Tormyle at play—but there was nothing childish in the stakes of the game it had engineered.

He said, "We have come for our friends."

"Those you seek are within the walls," said the hollow voice. "If you can enter, you may take them."

"If?"

"There are formalities. Customs to be observed. A ritual to be followed."

Chom snarled his anger. "More tests? Will the thing ever be satisfied? What more does it want us to do?"

"My brother!" Sac fought against Dumarest's restraining hand. "Let me go, Earl! Tek is waiting!"

He would have to wait a while longer. The game Tormyle had devised had to be conducted on the rules it had determined.

To the herald Dumarest said, "I don't understand what you mean. Explain."

"The explanation is obvious."

"Not to me."

"Earl!" Sac tore himself free and raced toward the lowered drawbridge. He reached it, put one foot on the planking and then spun as something buzzed from the darkness and enfolded him with gauzy wings. Still spinning, he fell as the shimmering creature vanished back into the darkness.

Ignoring him, Dumarest said, again, "Explain."

"That should not be necessary," boomed the herald. "You have a saying which provides all answers. Love will find a way. Therefore—find it!"

There was no food, no water, little shade and the temperature was rising all the time. From beneath the scant protection of the trees Dumarest stared thoughtfully at the castle. The herald had gone and the drawbridge had risen; all he could see were walls of stone, the towers, banners and the enigmatic glints of metal. A puzzle. A box containing the hostages. A stronghold which, somehow, he must find a way to enter.

He heard the rustle of movement and turned to find Daroca at his side.

"A peculiar construction, Earl." He nodded toward the castle. "I have been examining it too. Those towers seem to serve no useful purpose. See? They do not widen into overhangs so as to protect the base of the walls and they are too high to serve as viable platforms for archers. And who in their right senses would build a castle overlooked by the cliffs at the rear? The drawbridge, too; there is no moat or trench and so no need of such a bridge." He tilted his head, squinting. "My eyes are not as strong as they could be. Are those men on the walls?"

"An illusion," said Dumarest. "I've been watching them. A man would turn his head, alter his pace a little, be curious if nothing else. They aren't men." He added, with sudden impatience, "But we know that."

"True," admitted Daroca. "We are the only men on this world—us and those within the walls. But old habits die hard. We see a fragment of something familiar and fill in details from our own knowledge of what should be. A castle should contain armored men—therefore we see them. And yet the herald seemed real enough."

Real as the trees were real, the grass beneath their feet, as real as anything on this peculiar world. Dumarest turned and looked to where Sac Qualish was lying. The buzzing thing had rendered him unconscious; now Chom was cooling his forehead with a mass of leaves.

"He's coming round," he said as Dumarest stepped toward him. "He's stirred a couple of times and once he gave a groan." He lifted the leaves and used them as a fan to cool his own face. "What was it, Earl? The thing which attacked him? It looked like a giant butterfly to me."

"I thought it was a web," said Daroca. "Something like the mesh-symbiotes of Chemelophen. Not that it matters. The castle is obviously protected against direct attack."

Chom wiped his face and licked at his fingers, scowling at the taste of salt.

"First the cold," he grumbled. "That was to get us moving toward this end of the valley. Now the heat—how long can we last before taking some sort of action?"

"Not long," said Daroca. "But what kind of action can we take? Aside from illustrations I've never even seen a castle, much less learned how to take one. Earl?"

Sac groaned before Dumarest could answer. He stirred and sat upright, one hand to his head, his face creased with pain.

"What happened?" He frowned as they told him. "I remember something which buzzed, a sting as if I'd touched a live wire, and then nothing. You should have all followed me," he accused. "Together we might have been able to get inside the castle. Instead you were content to argue with that creature of Tormyle."

Chom said, "You talk like a fool. What did you gain by your action? What would any of us have gained? This is a time for thought, not stupid heroics." He threw aside the wad of leaves. "The herald spoke of customs, a ritual which should be followed. Have any of you any idea of what it meant?"

"It also said that love would find a way," reminded Dumarest.

The entrepreneur shrugged. "Maybe, but I am not in love."

"Not even with your own life?"

"That, perhaps." He rose, eyes shrewd in the rounded planes of his face. "A spur to the intelligence, you think? Find the answer or die in this heat? Daroca, you are a man of intelligence and one who claims to have studied many strange cultures. Can't you solve this riddle?"

As the man hesitated Dumarest said, "You spoke of chivalry and the concept of romantic love. Just what did you mean?"

"A legend, fable rather, but one based on fact. At least I think so. There was a time in some remote past, probably on a primitive world, when men built strongholds and wore armor and fought with simple weapons. They had a code of behavior which we know as chivalry. Kindness to the weak, help for the afflicted, adherence to a given word—a society which probably never existed but which the romantic wish to believe actually had. The legend probably arose from when men fought to exist on newly-settled worlds and had to band together against a common enemy. Something of the sort is to be found on Kremar and Skarl."

Dumarest was patient. "I know that. An aristocracy given to symbols and ritual. And the rest?"

"Romantic love?" Daroca shrugged. "An ideal based on a concept of purity. A man could love a woman for everything but the reason normal men love women. A distortion which placed high value on fetish instead of natural, sexual desire. A form of insanity, of course, but not without appeal to those who yearn for a reality which could never exist."

Chom made a sound of disgust. "Madness. And where could a thing like Tormyle gain such ideas? From Mari?"

"From Tek." Sac Qualish rose painfully to his feet. "As young men we were interested in old legends and codes of behavior. At one time we thought of writing a book based on stories which are enjoyed by children and which seem to be found on most worlds. Tales of great heroes and mighty deeds."

"And women who are more—or less—than human." Chom laughed. "You should have got married, Sac. A woman in the home would have cured such dreaming. But how does it help us to know all this? Will it help us scale those walls?" His broad hand gestured toward the crenellations, the glints of metal and streaming banners. "Destroy the things which are no doubt waiting for us?"

"You asked a question." The engineer was sullen. "I answered."

"With nonsense," snapped Chom. "With words when we need lasers and explosives."

"With ideas," corrected Dumarest. "With the answer we need."

Daroca looked his surprise. "Earl?"

"Tormyle is logical; we know that. Therefore this fantasy must contain elements of logic based on the things we see: a castle, banners, a herald wearing full armor. Tek's fantasy brought to life. Romantic love and what it means."

"I see." Daroca drew a deep breath. "You know," he said, "I think you've known all along what has to be done. The only thing which can be done. You knew, Earl. Admit it."

"Admit what?" Chom glared his bewilderment. "What are you talking about?"

"The way into the castle. The only way. Sac?"

The engineer was thoughtful. "A challenge. If all this is based on Tek's imaginings, then the castle will hold a champion. We must challenge him—it—and thus gain victory. But how can we do that?" He looked at what they carried, the crude weapons of wood and stone, remembering the armored creature on the horse, the thing which had buzzed and stolen his senses.

Dumarest said, "Chom, give me your club."

There was no sound as he walked toward the drawbridge. The soft ground muffled his boots so that he seemed to be walking on velvet. The heat now had grown so that the air quivered; breathing was a thing of conscious effort. Already they were suffering from the effects of dehydration; soon they would be too weak to do anything but lie and wait for death.

From above sang the single note of a trumpet.

Dumarest ignored it, concentrating on the planks of the drawbridge. As he got closer he could see anomalies—the planks were too exposed to fire, a thing never permitted in a real stronghold, and the ground lifted as it reached the walls instead of falling into a trench or moat. The walls, too, were seamless, the rough surface artificially streaked with what would have been mortared blocks. A facade, he thought, covering what? The rugged walls of the cliff perhaps. A cavern. A pit leading to the heart of this strange world. Anything which Tormyle desired. He could only trust in the logic of the machine and the determination of the thing to learn what it could never know.

The drawbridge was very close. He stepped to one side, cautious in case it should suddenly be lowered to crush him like an insect beneath the heel of a boot. Again the trumpet sounded and, as the clear note died, he sent the massive head of the club thundering against the wood. Twice more he beat the panel, hard, measured strokes, the stone gouging into the planks.

Something fell from above.

It buzzed, shimmering, twisting like a near-invisible skein of thread, bright colors shot with ebon, silver merging with scarlet. It shrilled and darted toward him, wide wings spread so as to engulf him, the buzzing higher and taut with menace.

Dumarest sprang backward, the club lifted, falling, lifting again to hammer once more at the wings, the shimmer, the tiny body he could see at the center of the mobile web.

As it squashed the buzzing died. For a moment the webs were still, multicolored lace spread on the sward and then, in a moment, both crushed body and wings had vanished.

From beneath the shelter of the trees he heard Chom's bellow of warning.

"Earl! The bridge! It's coming down!"

He sprang backward as the great slab of wood swept down from where it rested against the walls, reaching safety as the end jarred against the ground. Logic, he thought grimly. A double-edged weapon. Though there was no moat one was implied and, by beating against the structure, he had, in a sense, attacked the castle by frontal assault. The attack had been answered by the buzzing thing falling from above.

Three feet from the end of the drawbridge he stared at the dark opening, the fretted portcullis, the flanking walls of stone. A glimmer showed in the depths, the sound of hooves and the herald, magnificent in golden metal, advanced with lance at rest, the point aimed at his breast.

Dumarest said, "I challenge you!"

"Challenge?"

"You spoke of formalities, customs, a ritual to be observed. Send out your champion and let us fight. If I win, then the prisoners you hold are mine. The laws of chivalry demand that this be so."

The booming voice said, "You would fight me?"

"Yes."

"For love?"

"For life."

"The prime directive," mused the creature in the golden armor. "But why you, Earl? Why must it always be you? Have the others no desire to continue their existence? Or is your love for the woman so strong that it has overridden all caution and logical consideration? You will fight, you say. And the others?"

Dumarest said harshly, "Let us keep to the point. This is your game, Tormyle, your rules. Will you keep to them or not?"

For a long moment there was silence as if the thing were checking possibilities, weighing consequences, gauging the logic of the situation. And then, "I accept. In one hour we will fight."

Chapter

◆ TWELVE ◆

It was a long hour. The heat did not increase, for which Dumarest was thankful, but still the air remained oppressive, the sweat streaming from his body robbing him of precious salt. Sac, recovered, stared gloomily at the castle, his eyes narrowed as he tried to determine the nature of the enigmatic glints on the crenellated walls. Daroca too was wrapped in introspection, musing, his ringed hand lifting often to touch his cheeks, the lobe of his right ear. Only Chom was practical.

"That thing is armored, Earl. Wooden spears will be useless against the metal. Before you can use a club you'll have to get close, which means dodging the lance and whatever else it may be carrying. The bow?" He shrugged, thick shoulders heaving beneath his blouse. "How will you handle it, Earl?"

Sac said abruptly, "There! On that tower! Look!"

Dumarest followed his pointing hand and saw nothing but vagrant glimmers.

"He's gone. But I'm sure I saw him. Tek was standing watching. The others too."

Were they images created by imagination and the need to be reassured? Chom echoed his impatience.

"Dreaming won't help us. You're an engineer; can't you think of some way to help Earl defeat that creature?"

"No."

"Think, damn you! His life depends on it. All our lives. If you hope to save that brother of yours, quit staring and use your brain."

"I'm not a fighting man," said Sac dully. "I don't know anything about weapons. But what about the mount it

120

rides? Metal is heavy and if he could be thrown, it might help."

If it could be thrown. If the champion would be the herald. If it were a normal man with human limitations. Dumarest fought the inclination to regard it as anything more. If the champion was invulnerable, then he could not hope to win. But in that case there would be no point to the conflict. The rules of the game, he thought. The insane fantasy constructed by the world-intelligence must offer the hope of success or the entire experiment would be useless.

His knife whispered from his boot.

"Give me your blouse," he said to the engineer. "Daroca, search around and find me some stones. All you can get, any size, bring them to me here."

"Earl?"

"Do it!"

The knife sliced through the fabric of the blouse, cutting it into narrow strips which Dumarest plaited together to form three long cords which he joined together at one end. The stones Daroca had found were too small. His blouse yielded more material which Dumarest fashioned into pouches. He filled them with stones and lashed them to the free ends of the three cords. Rising, he spun the device over his head, faster, faster, releasing it to fly, spinning over the clearing to hit and wrap around the bole of a tree.

"Neat," said Chom as he unwrapped it. "Where did you learn to make a thing like that?"

"On Marakelle. They hunt small animals which are very fast." Dumarest jerked at the cords, tightening them and checking the pouches which held the stones. "A trained man can bring down a running beast at a hundred yards." He sorted other stones for use in the sling. Both weapons would serve to attack at a distance, but for close-quarter work he had nothing except the knife and the club. Neither were much use against an armored man.

"We could help," said Daroca abruptly. "If we all attack at the same time, it would make things easier. We could distract its attention if nothing else."

"No," said Sac.

"Why not? Are you afraid?"

"The challenge was for single combat. If Earl should be killed, then our turn will come." Again the engineer stared at the walls of the castle. "If Tormyle allows it. If it doesn't kill us all or let us die for want of food and water."

Chom said, "Stop talking about food and water. Earl will do his best; if he can't win, then we are as good as dead." His big hand ripped a mass of leaves from a tree. Wadding them, he thrust them into his mouth, chewed, then spat in disgust. "Nothing. Even the taste is vile. All you can do now, Earl, is to rest."

Rest and wait as he had done so often before during the moments before combat. To force himself to relax, to ease the tension which could weaken if maintained too long, the keen edge of concentration blunted by overstimulus. Dumarest lay in a patch of shade, eyes closed, apparently asleep but, as Chom knew, far from that. A man summoning his energies for violent action, a killing machine ready to explode.

From the castle came the sound of the trumpet.

"Now," whispered Daroca. He drew in his breath with a sharp hiss as the clear note sounded again. The drawbridge lowered and the champion rode from the darkness into the light of the glowing sky.

It was not the herald. It was not a thing of golden grace but big and broad, wearing black metal spined and curved in baroque monstrosity. The animal it rode was not a horse but a scaled thing with six legs and a long, prehensile tail. Jaws gaped, showing rows of savage teeth and fire spurting from the cavernous throat. A giant lizard or a dragon from fable, a part of the fantasy which Tormyle had constructed.

Chom sucked in his breath. "Earl! How the hell can you ever beat that?"

Dumarest watched as it came over the planking. The rider, cased all in black metal, carried a long lance, a mace, a sword and shield. A pennant fluttered from the lance, forked and bearing a device of red and yellow on a field of green. The thing itself, if constrained to human limitations, was no real danger. The armor would slow it down, the weapons it carried of use only at close quarters. The dragon was another matter.

It was green flecked with red, the scales limned with scarlet, the eyes, hooded by bony protuberances, gleaming like jewels. It was fast and quick and agile. The tail could swing like a club, the teeth rip like a hundred knives, the spurting flames burn and incinerate. Helpless before it he would be easy prey for the rider with his long lance.

Daroca said, "It's giving you no chance, Earl. None at all."

"We can't let him face it alone." Sac was trembling. "If we're going to die we may as well all go together."

Dumarest ignored the comments and checked his weapons, inflating his lungs. As the dragon and its rider reached the end of the drawbridge he stepped from beneath the shelter of the trees. He was ready as it came toward him over the soft ground.

The eyes were the only vulnerable point and, protected as they were, it wouldn't be easy to hit them. He stood, the loaded sling in his hands, judging time and distance. As the beast came closer he began to rotate the sling. It hummed through the air, making a thin, vicious sound. The dragon heard it and paused, head lifting, jaws gaping and bright with fire. The rider touched it with hooked spurs and the beast lowered its head, claws ripping at the dirt as it loped forward.

Dumarest waited, tense, concentrating on the glowing jewel of an eye, ignoring the gleaming tip of the lance, the teeth, the spurts of flame. The thongs of the sling were taut against his hand. One final turn and he released the stone, running as it left the pouch. He heard it hit, the soggy impact it made and then the dragon roared, head rearing, turning, blood streaming from the ruined eye.

Before the rider could regain control, Dumarest had raced forward, knocking the tip of the lance to one side, gripping it in both hands, and continued to run alongside the stricken dragon. Leverage did the rest. It was impossible for the rider to maintain its grip on the weapon without turning in the saddle and it could turn only so far. Dumarest tore it free, jumped over the lashing tail and ran another hundred yards before turning, lance in hand.

From the air Lolis whispered, "Well done, Earl. So very well done."

So far, perhaps, but the danger still remained. He had lost his sling, the thongs and pouch trampled and burned and the lance was poor exchange. He poised it as the dragon advanced, grounding the butt and aiming the point at the pulsing throat. An unthinking beast would have charged against it, but the dragon was more than that. Half blinded, fuming with rage, it had instilled cunning and the rider on its back recognized the danger. Dumarest felt a gush of fire and saw the wood of the shaft begin to smoke, the metal point glow with sudden heat. He ran as the tail lashed like a whip toward him. Turning, he threw the lance with all the power of his back and shoulders. It slammed into the side of the beast's neck and blood spurted from a gaping wound. Before it could recover he was spinning the bolas, the weights stretching the cords as he hurled it at the jaws. It hit, spun tight, cutting short the plumes of fire.

Then Dumarest was running forward again, reaching for the lance which had been shaken from the creature's neck, gripping it as the tail slammed against his side with numbing force. He rolled, fighting for air, seeing the clawed feet rise above him as the beast reared ready to rip out his intestines. A second and he would be dead—but a second was long enough. He crouched, lance upraised, the point burying itself into the scaled hide as the dragon crashed down, the metal shearing through flesh to impale the heart beneath.

Again the air whispered a compliment.

"So fast, Earl, so very fast. But you have not won yet."

The rider still remained. It had been thrown clear of the dying beast and now stood, grim in black plating, shield and sword ready for action. Against it Dumarest had nothing but his knife.

He circled warily, watching as the thing turned to face him. It was like a machine, a robot without discernible weakness, armed and armored against any attack. Dumarest lunged, the knife held like a sword, the point glittering as it swept toward the visor. The shield lifted, the sword hissed as it cut the air, the tip ripping the plastic of his blouse as Dumarest sprang back just in time.

Fast then, but careless, the creature should have used the point to thrust, not the edge to slash.

Again Dumarest lunged, leaping sideways as he feinted with the knife, forcing the thing to turn to guard its rear. He edged toward it, feinting, ducking, darting like a wasp at the armored shape, using his speed to avoid the sword, the slamming blows of the shield.

Then Dumarest sensed the dead creature at his side and turned, springing over it, stooping to tug at the lance. It was buried too deep. He released it as the sword whined down, the edge aimed at his head. He caught the blow on his knife, feeling the jar as he turned the blade. He snatched with his left hand at the mailed arm and threw himself backward as he gripped the limb.

Caught off balance, the armored figure toppled over the body of the dead beast. Before it could recover, Dumarest was on it, the knife in his hand stabbing at the visor, grating as it slipped through the eye-slits. Beneath him the figure heaved once and then was still.

Chom's voice roared in triumph.

"You have beaten it, Earl! You have won! The champion is dead and the prize is ours!"

But nothing was dead. Dumarest dragged free his knife and looked at the unstained blade. He jerked open the visor and saw nothing but emptiness within the helmet. A hollow man who had fought and would have killed, but could lose nothing in return.

Then the armor was gone, the dragon, the castle itself with the high walls and crenellations, the banners and soaring towers. The fantasy was over. Where it had stood was nothing but the merging cliffs of the valley.

And Mayenne.

She stood in a transparent cage, looking very small and helpless, her hair a glowing helmet of purest copper in the light from the shimmering sky. Beside her stood Karn, his eyes sunken, anxious. In an identical cage, yards distant, stood Mari and Tek Qualish.

Both cages were suspended on chains fastened to the ends of slender rods protruding from the cliff wall. Between them ran a narrow causeway at the far end of which was set a tall lever. To either side gaped an abyss.

Dumarest walked to the edge and looked down. The bottom was invisible. He looked to either side; there was no way to reach the cages aside from the causeway. The ground too had changed, the soft emerald of the sward replaced by a stony barrenness, the sparse trees once again the thick mass of vegetation they had previously known.

Chom came panting toward him, Sac and Daroca close behind.

"What new deviltry is this?" The entrepreneur scowled at the cages, the people within. "You won the bout, Earl. The prize should be ours now. Have we yet another test to pass?"

"Ingenious, isn't it?" Karn's voice came clearly from the confines of his cage. "A novelty devised by Tormyle. It told us all about it. You can save half of us—but only at the expense of the rest."

Dumarest stepped onto the causeway and examined the lever.

"Don't touch that!" said Karn sharply. "Not yet anyway."

"You'd better explain."

"Yes," said Karn. "We were meant to do just that." His arm made a vague gesture. "We're suspended, as you see. That lever will swing one cage to safety, depending on which way it is thrown. To the left, us; to the right, the others. The cage chosen will drop to the causeway and open. The other will fall into the abyss. I don't have to tell you what will happen to the occupants if it does."

"Mayenne?"

"It is as he says, Earl. We two against the others. You have to decide." She paused and added, "There is a time limit. Ten thousand heartbeats. At the end of that time both cages will fall."

Over two hours, more than enough time for thought. Beside Dumarest, Sac Qualish whimpered like a dog.

"I don't believe it! Tek, she's lying, isn't she? She has to be lying."

His brother was calm. "No."

"Mari?"

"She's telling the truth as it was given to us."

Dumarest said, "Is there any way you can get out of those cages? Is there anything we can do to get you out?"

"No." Karn was positive. "I've been over every inch of it."

"Tek?"

"We're in sealed boxes. As far as I can make out both cages are solid." His calmness was unnerving, the resignation of a man who had accepted the inevitable. "As Mayenne said, it's for you to decide."

A decision no man should ever have to make, Dumarest thought. As Sac edged toward the lever Dumarest said, "We must think about this. Discuss it. I suggest we all sit in the shade."

"No," said the engineer. "I'll stay here."

"You'll do as Earl says." Chom closed his big hand over the other's arm. "We'll gain nothing standing in this heat. Come now. You too, Daroca. We'll go back to where we watched the fight."

Back beneath the trees Daroca slumped against a bole, Chom squatting like a toad at his side. The entrepreneur frowned at the suspended cages.

"It must have got that idea from Mari. Some houses of pleasure specialize in displaying their wares in such a fashion. The rest? Well, Karn would know about opposed balances, Tek also."

"And cruelty?" Daroca forced himself to sit upright with an obvious effort. The man was dying, thought Dumarest dispassionately. They would all die unless the temperature fell and food and water was provided. "This shows a refinement usually only to be found in highly sophisticated cultures. An application of mental torment. Who is to decide and how? No matter who is chosen, the winner will also lose. It will not be pleasant to carry the memory of those he has doomed to extinction."

"Nobody is dead yet," said Dumarest. "And perhaps nobody will die. You're an engineer, Sac. Is there any way we can lock the mechanisms?"

"Without being able to study it, how can I tell?"

"You could try. Even I know that a stone in the right place could wreck any machine ever built. No," he said sharply as Sac made a move toward the causeway. "I don't want you to touch anything. Not yet."

"Don't you trust me?"

Dumarest made no answer and looked instead at the

cages, the abyss and the causeway. With fire they could
burn down trees and set the boles so as to prevent the
cages from falling. With rope they could lash them fast in
some way. But they had no rope and no time to make it
and they would never be able to fell trees in time.

"A problem," said Chom musingly. "And one of which I
am glad to have no part. You, Earl, are concerned with
the Ghenka. You, Sac, with your brother. Only one can be
saved. Perhaps you had better draw lots to decide which."

"No," said Sac.

"Fight then? You would be foolish to do that. Earl
would surely win."

Dumarest said flatly, "There will be none of that. We
didn't fight our way here to kill each other at Tormyle's
whim. I have another suggestion."

Daroca stirred. "Which is?"

"We do nothing."

"And let them all die?" Sac stared disbelievingly. "No. I
can't agree to that. Damn it, Earl; you forget that Tek is
my brother!"

"And you forget that if it hadn't been for Earl you
would be dead," snapped Chom.

"I've not forgotten. But I'm alive and so is Tek. I want
to keep him that way."

Daroca said quietly, "I suggest we lower our voices. It
can't be pleasant for those in the cages to hear our discussion. Now, Earl, what did you mean when you suggested
that we do nothing?"

"What else can we do? Fight? Kill half in order to save
the others? We've jumped to Tormyle's tune long enough.
Each test we've faced has been followed by another. Now
I say it's time to call a halt. We sit and do nothing. If it
wants to kill us all, there is nothing we can do to stop it.
But I'm damned if I'm going to cater any longer to its sadistic pleasure."

"A bluff," said Chom shrewdly. "Is that what you think,
Earl?"

"I don't know. I hope so."

"You hope?" Sac stared at his clenched hands. "Is that
all?"

"You know the alternative."

"Tek alive and the others dead. Yes, I know it, but Tek will be alive. Alive, do you hear? Alive!"

"Be silent!" snapped Daroca. "Remember they can hear you!"

"I don't care if they can!" The man was almost hysterical. With an effort he forced himself to speak more quietly. "Listen, Earl. I owe you my life and I won't forget it. Anything I can give you is yours for the asking. But not this. Damn it, man; you can always get another woman. I can never get another brother."

"Logic," said Chom blandly. "And I am sure that we all appreciate it. So let us be logical. I was wrong when I said that I had no interest in this problem. I had forgotten the captain and, as we are being logical, he must be considered. Of what use to save the others if we have no one who is capable of handling the ship? Of them all Karn is the most important and the fact that the Ghenka is with him is a happy accident for Earl. Save one and you save both, and the captain must be saved if we are ever to leave this insane world. My regrets, Sac, but it seems your brother must be sacrificed for the common good."

"No one will be sacrificed," said Dumarest sharply.

Chom shrugged. "No? You are one man, Earl, among four. I vote for the captain. Daroca?"

"I say we wait and do nothing."

"Two to wait, one to save the captain. It seems, Sac, that you are in a minority." Chom added softly, "Unless, of course, you decide to side with me."

Dumarest said, "There will be no decisions. If any of you choose to commit murder then you will be the first to die. Now sit down, Sac, and relax. There is nothing to do but wait."

"We can talk." The engineer moved toward the stony ground. "There are things I'd like to say to my brother—and have you nothing to say to Mayenne?"

He spun as Dumarest glanced toward her, swinging the club he had snatched up to smash at the unprotected skull. Dumarest caught the movement and threw himself aside in time to avoid the full impact of the blow. Instead of crushing bone and brain it glanced off the side of his head, sending him to his knees, half stunned, blinded with pain.

He heard Daroca cry out, Chom's voice exploding in a

curse and the rasp of boots against rubble. He staggered to his feet, right hand lifting with the knife. Then he dropped it as he realized the impossibility of the throw. Already Sac was at the causeway and racing toward the lever at the far end. Quickly he scooped up a stone and threw it with the full strength of his arm. It hit the running man between the shoulders, sending him sprawling, his outstretched hands touching the lever. He rose as Dumarest reached for another stone. As he poised it to throw he heard the deep thrum of a string, the vicious hiss of an arrow.

Sac cried out, lifting his hands to the shaft buried in his throat, twisting, falling, the weight of his body hitting the lever.

It was thrown toward the left.

Chapter

◆ **THIRTEEN** ◆

Chom laughed and tore at the smoking meat, filling his mouth so that juices ran down his chin. He chewed and swallowed and reached for wine, filling a goblet full of lambent gold.

"Come, my friends," he said. "Let us celebrate. Tormyle has been most kind."

Food for the rats, thought Dumarest bleakly, comforts as a reward for successful endeavor. A house had appeared from nowhere, a table loaded with meats and fruits, wine and a dozen varieties of pastry. The entrepreneur was enjoying himself.

"Come," he said again. "Earl, Mayenne, all of you. Eat, drink and be glad that you are alive. A song later, maybe, after other matters have been taken care of." His leer left nothing to the imagination. "I'll be content with simpler pleasures. Synthetic as it may be, this meat is the finest I've ever tasted. The wine also."

Daroca nibbled fastidiously. Karn chewed with a vague abstraction as if his thoughts were elsewhere. Mayenne sipped at some wine.

"Earl?"

She wanted to talk, to relive the episode, to feel again, perhaps, the relief she had known when her cage had swung to safety. Dumarest preferred to leave things where they belonged among the dead memories of the past.

"Eat," he said. "You must be starving."

She frowned. "Why do you say that? We ate only a short while ago. At the ship, remember?"

Time, he thought. Moments for her had been hours for

131

them. Had she been kept in some form of stasis? It didn't matter. Not now.

"Earl," she said. "I must know. I heard you talking while I was in the cage. Would you really have sat and waited and done nothing?"

The truth would have hurt. He said, "Does it matter?"

"No," she admitted. "Not now. But I wonder what would have happened if Sac hadn't forced a decision. Would we all have died? Would Tormyle have repented?"

He moved, restless in his chair, conscious of the futility of the discussion. Conscious too of other things. Chom was celebrating, using their assumed victory as an excuse to eat and guzzle wine, but they had really won nothing but a respite.

"Poor Sac," said Mayenne after a moment. "And his brother. Mari too. They didn't deserve to die as they did. Killed for nothing at all."

Dumarest said, "Don't think about it."

"I won't," she promised. "But you saved my life, Earl. I shall never forget that."

"Thank Daroca, not me. He fired the arrow which killed Sac."

"Daroca?" Leaning forward, she touched his hand. "I must thank you," she said. "For what you did. It was a wonderful shot. Bad for Mari and Tek, but good for me and Karn. Earl too," she added. "I will never give him cause to regret your skill with a bow."

He reached for wine, sipped and said, "I wish I could take the credit, Mayenne, but I didn't use the bow. I lacked the strength to pull the string. It was Chom who shot the arrow."

Chom? Dumarest looked at where he sat, a man who had denied all skill with a bow. A lucky shot, perhaps? It was a facile answer, but not good enough. Until now he had assumed Daroca had killed Sac but, if so, why had he denied it?

Karn sighed and said to no one in particular, "How can I explain? When we get back to Ayette, what can I tell them? All those passengers dead, the captain, the ship delayed."

Chom blinked his amazement. "That worries you?"

"They will want to know." Karn was insistent, clinging, Dumarest realized, to familiar routine, familiar problems.

"Tell them the truth," said Chom.

"You think they will believe it?"

"They will have no choice. You have witnesses and can pass any test they may devise for the determination of truth. But why go to Ayette at all? The galaxy is wide, my friend, and now you have a ship of your own. With some adjustment I'm sure that none of us will complain if you chose to open a fresh trading route. Partners, maybe?" Chom smiled at the thought. "A regular income, comfort assured for old age, a nice home on some nice world. What do you say, Earl?"

"Karn has his duty."

"And duty is sacred?" The entrepreneur shrugged and reached for more wine. "We have only one life, my friend. We owe it to ourselves to spend it as best we may. Karn would be a fool to waste his opportunities. You agree, Daroca?"

"It is a philosophy I have heard before."

"So short of words?" Chom lowered his goblet and thrust aside his plate. "What's the matter with you all? We have come through great dangers and have won the test and all you can do is to sit and brood. Tormyle has proved to be generous." His hand waved at the house in which they sat. "Soon we shall be on our way with a ship and a galaxy to rove in. There are worlds I know on which we could do well. Contract labor for the mining planets, for example. Peasants who would sign away their lives for cheap passage. Cargoes which the squeamish hesitate to touch. All ours for the taking. And, friends, ours by right. We are the victors and to us go the spoils." He beamed and Dumarest realized that he was more than a little drunk. "How about it, Daroca?"

"Do as you please—once I have landed on a civilized world."

"You then, Earl. Of us all you have the greatest right. You are truly the victor."

"Of what?" said Dumarest harshly. "Of meat and wine and a place to sleep ? Or are you thinking of the dead?"

"They are gone," said Chom. "We are alive. Come, Earl, let us drink to that at least."

"Go to hell," said Dumarest, and rose from the table.

Mayenne followed him outside to where the shimmering sky threw its monotonous light. The abyss had closed; the mechanisms of the test had vanished. Now there was nothing but the merging cliffs and the stony ground at their feet. The temperature had fallen so now it was like a pleasant summer's afternoon on a gentle world.

He turned. The house was low, rambling, a place of colonnades and pointed windows, fretted woodwork and peaked roofs. Over it hung trees bearing scented blossoms and flowers glowed in profusion on all sides.

"It's beautiful," whispered Mayenne. "Earl, darling, if we could only have a house like this for our own, how happy I would be. There would be room for guests and parlors in which we could entertain. And other rooms where children would be safe. Our children, Earl. I am not too old to give you sons."

And daughters who would sing as their mother sang. A home which would be his and the things most men regarded as important. A fair exchange, perhaps, for his endless quest for a lost world. For the empty travel and strange planets and the bleak life in ships which traversed the void.

He turned and faced her and saw the bronze of her hair, the smooth lines of her face, the eyes, jet with their smoldering flecks of ruby. He reached out and touched her and felt the life throbbing beneath her skin, the blood and bone and sinew which made her shape, the softness he remembered so well. Human and warm and vulnerable. He felt a sudden wave of protective tenderness and held her close as if to shield her from all harm.

"Earl?" She looked up at him and gently touched his cheek. "Darling, is something wrong?"

She had recognized the embrace for what it was. He forced himself to smile.

"No."

"Don't lie to me, Earl. I can feel it when you do."

"Nothing is wrong."

She was eager to be convinced and relaxed, smiling as she stepped back from his arms.

"I think it's time we were alone, darling. I have picked our room; it is a beautiful place. Let me show it to you."

"Later."

She did not argue, sensing with her woman's intuition his desire to be alone. Instead she said, "It is the third on the left past the room in which we ate. You will not be long?"

"No."

Daroca emerged as she entered the house. He looked after her for a moment, then walked to where Dumarest stood beneath the scented trees.

"A beautiful woman, Earl. You will never know how much I envy you." He paused and then, as Dumarest made no comment, said, "A stupid remark, but old habits die hard and much of my life has been spent in making banal conversation. Yet I was sincere. She loves you and will make you happy."

Dumarest said, "Perhaps."

"You doubt her? No. Something else, then?" He frowned as Chom's voice came booming through the open door. "Listen to that fool. He is trying to talk Karn into turning pirate or slaver, but he is wasting his time. Our captain is a man of honor. He will do his duty no matter what the personal cost."

"You are tired," said Dumarest. "You should eat and rest."

"Later, when my mind has quieted. Now, each time I close my eyes, I am back on that cliff riding your back to safety. And there is something else. Chom thinks that our ordeal is over. I am not so sure, and, I think, neither are you."

"No," said Dumarest bleakly. "I don't think that it is over."

He woke and knew immediately that something was wrong. He turned, reaching, but found only emptiness beside him. Mayenne was gone, the room in which they had slept, the window framing the scented trees. Instead he lay on a couch of some soft material in a room all of gold and crystal with cerise carpet on the floor and his clothes lying on a chair. Quickly he dressed and commenced to search. A door opened on a bathroom, another on a kitchen, a third on a long, low open space with a floor of polished wood and small tables bearing statues, ornaments, flowers caught in transparent blocks. A montage of things he had known before, assembled—where?

"Do you like it, darling?"

"Mayenne!"

He turned, quickly, staring at the figure at the end of the room. The light was subdued and he had been misled by the lilt in the voice. It was not Mayenne.

"You," he said. "Tormyle."

She smiled and came closer, dressed as he had seen her at the stream, the diaphanous gown parting to reveal soft and glowing flesh. There were alterations. The face was not quite as he remembered. Lolis had been beautiful, but young and with a certain vacuity. Now that touch of emptiness had gone. The hair too was different, glowing with the sheen of bronze, and the figure was more mature. The voice also. A blend, he thought, something of Mayenne added to Lolis. A composite.

"I asked if you like it, darling." Her hand gestured to the room, the apartment. "I made it just for you."

"As a cage?"

"As a place where we can talk. You would prefer that I whispered from a leaf? My shape to be something else? Earl, why do you fight against me? I want to be your friend."

He said bitterly, "You have an odd way of showing it."

"Because of the trials to which you were put? But, Earl, I had to make sure. I had to be positive. The experiment had to be carried to its logical conclusion. You would care for some wine?"

"No."

"Why not? You drink with the woman, why not with me?"

He caught the sharpness, the note of petulance, and frowned. Mayenne had been jealous and he had wondered why the alien should have adopted a female shape. The test, also, had contained elements of willfulness which would have been alien to a true machine. And yet what else could the thing be?

He said, "Can you drink?"

"But of course!" Her laughter was music. "Do you think

this shape is like those I sent against you in the valley? Earl, my darling, I build well. This body is totally functional. See?" She stretched and turned so as to display her curves. A decanter stood on a table and she poured two glasses of wine, swallowing hers without pause. "I can drink and eat and do everything a female of your species can do."

"Bleed?"

"That also." She came close and held out her arm. "Cut me if you wish. Use your knife against me. Kill me if it pleases you."

He could do it. He could slam his knife into her heart, but how long would she remain dead? Even if he managed to destroy the shape before him, how could it affect the planetary being?

"You don't want to hurt me," she said, and lowered her arm. "You are gentle, Earl, and kind, and you think of others. You have shown me what love really is."

He reached for his wine and sipped cautiously, wetting his lips while pretending to swallow. He felt the prickle of danger as if he stood at the edge of an invisible chasm in utter darkness. A thing not seen but sensed with the instinctive caution which had more than once saved his life.

"Love," she mused. "Such a complex emotion, as you once told me, Earl. And it comes in so many different forms. The love of a man for his brother, for his companions, an emotion strong enough for him to risk his life. The love of a man for a woman. A woman for a man. A passion strong enough to make him kill. Never before have I experienced such a thing. Once I would have thought it madness."

Dryly he said, "There are those who would agree with you."

"But not you, Earl."

"In some cases, yes."

"No. Such an emotion would not be love as you have taught me it should be. Greed, maybe, the desire to possess, a yearning to fulfill a personal need, but it would not be true love."

She had learned, he thought, and perhaps learned too well. He toyed with his wine, conscious of his inadequacy. He could have sensed a real woman's mood and played on it, appealing to her pride and intelligence, manipulating words and meanings to achieve a desired end. But a woman would have had obvious motives none of which could be applied to Tormyle. This thing beside him, no matter how she appeared, was not a woman but the manifestation of a planetary intelligence.

"You admit that we have answered your question," he said. "The thing you wanted to know."

"Yes, Earl."

"Then when can we leave?"

A couch stood against one wall. She moved toward it and gestured him to join her. As he seated himself, she said, "Why are you in so much of a hurry, Earl? I have provided for your friends. They have comfort and pleasant surroundings."

"It isn't enough. Men aren't animals to be satisfied with food and a comfortable prison."

"Other comforts, then? A larger house, a greater variety of food, entertainment which could amuse and please?"

Putting down his wine, Dumarest said, "You said the ship had been repaired and we made a bargain. We have kept our side of it. When are you going to keep yours?"

"Later, Earl."

"You will let us go?"

Her laughter was music. "Of course, my darling. You worry over nothing. But not yet. I have waited so long for novelty, do you begrudge me a little now that I have the chance to enjoy it?"

He said flatly, "More fights, Tormyle? More tests? More tricks to amuse you?"

"No." She moved against him, coming very close, her thigh touching his so that he could feel the softness of her flesh, the warmth of her body. A real woman would have felt like that, but she wasn't real. Always he must remember that. She wasn't real.

As if reading his thoughts, she said, "Touch me, Earl. Hold me. Close your eyes and be honest. Can you tell the difference between me and that other?"

He could, but he knew better than to say so.

"Can you imagine what my life has been?" she asked softly. "The long, so long, empty years. Always alone. I didn't realize how much alone until you came. Now things can never be the same as they were. I have seen what life can really be like, the interplay of emotion, the sense of companionship, the sharing. Can you understand, Earl? Can you even begin to guess what it means? The ability to talk to someone as I talk to you. The knowledge that there is something wonderful which I can share. To love and be loved. To belong to someone. To have another entity care for me so strongly that he would kill and die for my sake. You have it. To you it is a normal part of existence, but I have never known it until now. I want it, my darling. I want it and you can give it to me. You must!"

He said, very carefully, "Me?"

"You, Earl."

"I don't understand, Tormyle. What can I give you that you don't already have?"

She reached out to touch his shoulder and turned him so as to stare into his face. Her hair caught the light in metallic shimmers, bronze, beautiful, as were her face, her eyes.

"You are not a fool, Earl. You understand well enough. But if you want me to say it I will. I love you, darling. I love you—and I want you to love me in return."

Chapter
◆ FOURTEEN ◆

Vast caverns filled with crystalline growths, endless tunnels through which ran conductive fluids, the blazing heart of atomic fires; the brain, the veins, the heart of a planetary being. The control of tremendous forces were the hands which could reach across space, move worlds, tear apart the hearts of suns.

A world demanding to be loved.

Dumarest was thinking in mechanistic terms and that was wrong. Tormyle wasn't simply a gigantic artifact. There was more, a life-form in its own right, an intelligence which was too vast to comprehend. It was better to sit and look at the female shape and think of her as a woman with a woman's needs: to meet her on those terms and deal with her as he could.

He said casually, "You have learned more than I guessed, Tormyle. It seems now that you also have a sense of humor."

"Earl?"

"Surely you must be joking."

"You think that? No, darling, I'm serious. And would it be so hard for you to love me? If this shape doesn't please you, there are others I can wear. Shapes without number. And there is more I can offer. Think of what you desire and it will be yours. See?"

The apartment dissolved and became a great hall filled with bowing courtiers, creatures fashioned to obey his dictates. The hall opened to show fields of crops, houses, snaking roads filled with traffic. Mountains reared, golden, glittering with gems. They sank into an ocean filled with strange fish and on which armadas sailed. Ten thousand

140

women danced in the silver light of a sky filled with lambent moons.

All his for the price of love.

More power than any man had ever dreamed of. A world for his plaything in which he would rule as a king. A god.

A pet.

He lifted his wine as the apartment returned, his hand shaking a little as he drank, deeply this time, quenching more than a physical thirst. Every man had his need for heaven and she had shown him that and more. But at a price.

Unsteadily he said, "You offer much, perhaps too much, and I am overwhelmed. But you forget. I am mortal and will age. You will grow bored. What then?"

"I will never grow bored, Earl. Not with your love."

"And the rest?"

"Your age?" She laughed, triumphant. "Such a little thing. My darling, I can take your mind and the pattern which makes you unique and I can store it in a part of my being. You will never die. Your body, the shape you wear, may age, but then it can be replaced. We shall be together for an eternity, Earl. Always together. Always in love."

A girl in the grip of her first love affair making promises impossible to keep. For a year, ten perhaps, and then the novelty would fade. She would become impatient with his limitations and he would become, at the best, a tolerated pet; at the worst, a thing to be eliminated. Even if neither happened, what would happen to his pride?

He rose and moved restlessly about the room. It was warm, comfortable, but it had no door and no matter how pleasant a place it was still a prison. As the entire planet was a prison and one from which he had to escape.

He said, "You don't need me."

"That is nonsense, darling."

"You will forget," he said. "After we have gone, all this will diminish in importance. An interesting experiment which has yielded a new fact, no more. You feel this way because you have put too much of yourself in a female shape. You have built too well. Change and you will no longer feel the same. Love is not as you think. It can't be switched on. It is something founded in shared hardship,

suffering and even pain. Unending joy would sicken and
cloy by repetition. Surely you understand that."

She sat very still and when she spoke there was no
laughter in her voice.

"You refuse me?"

Carefully he tried to soften the fact. "Not refuse. Not
in the way you mean. But I am a man and you are a
world. What could there be in common between us? You
can give me everything I wish, true; but what can I give
you? Protection? You don't need it. Comfort? How can
that be possible? Companionship? I can't even begin to understand the complexity of your being. As I said, you
don't need me."

"You are wrong, Earl. So very wrong. I need the one
thing I cannot otherwise obtain. The thing which you
alone can give."

An obsession, he thought, or perhaps the culmination of
an experiment in which he was an integral part. Or it
could be that he was observing the symptoms of a growing
aberration. There was no way to be sure. He could be
cunning and agree to do as she asked. With a normal
woman who held him in her power that is what he would
have done: given lip service and waited for an opportunity
to escape. But how could he ever free himself from the
tyranny of a planetary intelligence?

He said flatly, "What you ask is impossible. I can't love
a world."

"You must stop thinking of me like that, Earl," she insisted. "I am a woman."

"If you were I would kill you. For what you did out
there in the valley."

"The experiment?" She shrugged. "Certain things had to
be determined. The girl, for example. You care for her.
But why her and not me? How am I different from that
entity for whom you risked your life?"

He said harshly, "Isn't that obvious? You have experienced none of the normal things which go to make a person. You are a beautiful pretense and nothing more.
Damn it, you aren't even human."

"And if I were?"

He hesitated, sensing danger, conscious that he had already said too much. A woman scorned could be a vicious

enemy and she was acting like a jealous woman, a woman determined to get her own way no matter what the cost. And he knew how ruthless she could be.

It was a time for lies.

"If you were it would be different. You are lovely, as you know, and any man would be proud to call you his own. But you are not human and we both know it." He added regretfully, "It is something I cannot forget."

"But if I were a real woman, Earl, as frail as you, as mortal?"

"Perhaps."

"And if I could bear you sons?"

He almost smiled at the impossibility, but this was no game, no pleasant bandying of words.

"Certainly. But that is beyond reason. Why don't you prove your love and let us go?"

"Perhaps I will, Earl," she said softly. "Perhaps I will go with you. You would like that. You and I together, sharing, enjoying all the things which lovers do. It can be done, Earl. You know that."

He tensed, sensing the closing jaws of a trap. Carefully he said, "I cannot begin to understand the full extent of your powers, Tormyle, but even you can't become wholly human."

"No?" Her laughter held a hint of mockery. "You know better than that, Earl. There is a way and you know it. You will give it to me, as a token of your love."

The apartment vanished. Abruptly he was in the open air, staggering a little from the sudden shock of transition, catching his balance as the ground seemed to move beneath his feet. Before him the house quivered, then dissolved into streamers of colored smoke. From within the mist he heard Chom's startled roar.

"The meat! The wine! What is happening?"

A gust of air blasted away the mist. Dumarest felt the pressure on his back and turned to see the great bulk of the ship standing at the end of the valley where the cages had hung suspended from their chains. It had been moved to this place by the power of Tormyle.

He heard Karn cry out and saw him running toward the ship. Daroca stared and headed toward him, Chom at his heels. Mayenne passed them both. She was shaking, her face wet with tears.

"Earl! I thought you were dead. When I woke and found you gone I didn't know what to do."

"We looked everywhere," said Daroca. "But I guessed what had happened. Tormyle?"

"Yes."

"A long, cozy chat?" said Chom. "A deal, maybe?"

"We talked, yes."

"About her letting us go?" Chom rubbed his hands. "I wish I could have joined the conversation. A woman like that, crazy for love, how often does a man get such a chance? You took advantage of it, of course. Used your attraction to get us free. A bonus too, perhaps? A cargo of precious metal to help us on our way? Food, at least; that meat was delicious."

Daroca said, "Chom, you disgust me. What happened, Earl? Has anything been decided?"

"I'm not sure."

"But you spoke?"

"Yes, and something was decided, but I am not sure exactly what."

He remembered the girl, the words she had used, the thin spite in her voice at the last, that and the expression of triumph in her eyes. Human emotions for an alien being, too human, and he wondered if it had all been part of an act. There had been something else too, a note of conviction that, in this game they were playing, she would surely win.

And he would help her do it.

Karn came back toward them from the ship. He looked distraught.

"It's still sealed," he said. "I don't understand it. Why should Tormyle have brought the ship here, if it didn't intend us to leave? Damn it, we did what it wanted; why can't it play fair?"

"You credit it with a sense of justice it doesn't possess," said Daroca, "and ethics it couldn't understand. Fair play is a uniquely human attribute. It is a voluntary sense of duty toward another which dictates that it is moral to keep a promise. It isn't even universal. On Krag, for example, there is a culture which has no time for such softness. They think it a mark of insanity. On that world it is normal to lie and cheat and steal."

"Philosophy," Chom sneered. "At a time like this we have to listen to your spouting. You said that I disgusted you, Daroca; well, you sicken me. It is all very well for the wealthy to prate of ethics, but when you've had to snatch a living from the dirt you have no time for such luxuries."

"I hardly call acting like a civilized human being a luxury."

The entrepreneur shrugged. "What does it mean to be civilized? To live in houses and obey laws and consider others? There are harsher jungles in cities than are to be found on primitive worlds. A code of ethics, then? If Tormyle said that all could leave but one and that one was you, Daroca, would you be willing to sacrifice yourself? If it chose another, Earl perhaps, would you insist that he stayed?"

"That is an academic question."

"Is it?" Chom's eyes were shrewd. "Perhaps it is, but there has to be some reason why we still cannot leave. Is that what happened, Earl? Was an offer made?"

"No."

"If it came to that, would you be willing to stay so that we could leave?"

"He wouldn't stay alone," said Mayenne. "I would never leave without him."

"Love," said Chom. "Madness. To hell with it. Karn, let's see if we can get into that ship somehow."

The ports were sealed as they had been before. Dumarest examined them, frowning. Chom and the officer slammed heavy stones against the locks. The metal resisted the impact. Chom swore as a stone split in his hands, and he flung aside the pieces.

"There has to be a way," he stormed. "We are intelligent beings with brains and imagination. A lock is nothing but a strip of metal—surely we can find a way to break it. Karn, can't we get in through the vents?"

"Without tools, no."

"Explosives?" Chom was clutching at straws. "A ram of some kind?"

A hammer was the best they could devise. Dumarest

swung the long shaft made from a sapling he had cut
down with his knife. The head was a great stone lashed
with strips of cloth. Three times he slammed the weight
against the port, denting the metal before the lashings
broke and the stone fell to one side. Panting, chest heaving from the effort of manipulating the heavy weight, he
watched as Karn checked the lock.

"It's still fast," he said. "I don't think we can get in this
way."

"We can try," snapped Chom. "Stop worrying about the
damage to your precious vessel and help me repair the
hammer."

At Dumarest's side Mayenne said quietly, "It isn't over
yet; is it, Earl? If Tormyle was willing for us to leave,
why should the ship still be sealed?"

"An oversight, perhaps." He was deliberately casual.
"Or perhaps a final test. If we are intelligent we should be
able to gain entry."

"We couldn't before."

"Our motives were different. Then we wanted weapons
and shelter. Now we are all together and want to leave.
Once we hammer in that port our troubles will be over."

He watched as Chom lifted the repaired hammer, thick
shoulders heaving as he lifted the weight. He took two
steps toward the port and halted, pressing at the air.

Karn said sharply, "What is wrong?"

"I don't know." Chom grunted as he pushed forward,
the hammer falling from his hands. "Daroca?"

"It's a barrier," he said wonderingly. "Invisible, soft, but
I can't pass. It seems to be all around the ship."

"Not the ship," said Karn. He had been investigating.
"About us."

It circled them in a cylinder of confining energy through
which they could see the trees, the cliffs and the ship now
more remote than ever before. Dumarest looked at the
others where they had spread to determine its perimeters.
As he watched they fell toward each other, pushed by the
relentless pressure he felt at his back, moving to halt in a
circle ten feet in diameter. He lifted his hand. Two feet
above his head he felt resistance. Stooping, he thrust his
knife at the soil. It halted an inch below the surface.

"Earl?" Mayenne's eyes reflected her fear as she caught at his arm. "What is happening?"

"We're in a box."

"Another cage? But why, Earl? What does it hope to gain by tormenting us like this?"

In his ear a voice whispered.

"Earl, my darling, now you will give me the means to make us one. A gift to prove your love. Act quickly or it will be too late to save your friends." A pause and then, *"Your friends, darling—and yourself."*

The wall thickened and became opaque; only the low ceiling remained transparent and permitted the entry of light. Karn moved restlessly about the area.

"I don't like this," he complained. "I don't understand it."

"A test," Daroca mused. "Another device of Tormyle's, but to prove what? Earl, did it give you any clue as to what it intends?"

Dumarest made no answer as he probed at the walls, the ceiling, the soil beneath their feet. The barrier had solidified so that he felt what seemed to be marble, hard, cold to the touch.

Mayenne said, "Look! Something's happening!"

Four feet above the ground, hard against the curved wall, a panel had appeared, an oblong board with fifteen buttons in glowing scarlet each marked with a familiar symbol.

Chom said, "What is it? A combination lock of some kind? Are we supposed to solve the correct sequence in order to get out?"

"Those are the signs of molecular units," said Karn blankly. "I studied biochemistry once. But what are we supposed to do with them? Earl, do you know?"

He knew too well. They were to be arranged, set in the correct sequence for the production of the affinity-twin, the secret he had carried and guarded for so long. Dumarest looked at the bright roof and enclosing walls and recognized the trap for what it was. The enclosed space was small; the air could not last for very long. Sooner or later he would have to operate the lock and release them—and give Tormyle the secret.

To be used—how?

"These buttons are loose," said Daroca. He stood before the panel, touching them, the great ring on his finger glowing with reflected light. "They can be taken out and replaced and, obviously, they have to be rearranged in a certain order. But which?"

He began to move them, setting them in various combinations, his long fingers deft as he worked. Dumarest watched, his face impassive. The chance that Daroca could hit on the correct sequence was remote, but it existed and he could afford to wait.

"This is useless," said Daroca after a while. "There are too many possible combinations. Perhaps we have to set them in an order which has some relevance to biochemistry. Karn, you said you knew something about it. Is there an organism or a creature which would contain these elements in a peculiar order?"

"They are elemental building materials for organic life, but that is all I know." Karn scowled at them, bending close as if to study the markings in greater detail. He moved a few of the buttons at random, then shrugged. "There is nothing I can do to help. You might as well carry on."

"The air's getting thicker," said Chom. "Hurry."

It was imagination, thought Dumarest. The air could not be getting stale so soon. Then something caught at his throat and he heard Karn's incredulous shout.

"Gas! The place is filling with gas!"

Dumarest coughed, retching, his nose and lungs filled with the stench of chlorine. Mayenne doubled and fell, her eyes enormous as she fought to breathe. Daroca fell back from the panel, one of the buttons falling from his hand.

Dumarest scooped it up and faced the panel. He had no time for thought or for the testing of the possibility of a bluff. He was dying, they were all dying, and only his knowledge could save them. The last button clicked home.

The gas vanished. The opaque wall, the glowing ceiling. Only the panel remained, falling to lie face upward on the ground beneath the shimmering sky.

He dived for it, coughing. His eyes streamed as he reached for the buttons and tore them free, scattering them to either side.

Rising, he faced Tormyle.

Chapter

◆ FIFTEEN ◆

She was more beautiful than before, with subtle changes that likened her more than ever to Mayenne. But the Ghenka held a human warmth and slight imperfections while Tormyle was the personification of an ideal.

Chom sucked in his breath in naked admiration.

"My lady," he said. "This is indeed an honor. Never before have I seen a woman so rare."

She ignored the compliment, looking at Dumarest. "I must thank you for your gift, my darling. You see how easily I am pleased? Now, soon, I shall be wholly a woman, one able to bear you sons."

Her voice matched her face and her body, singing like music.

"What does it mean, Earl?" Mayenne came to his side, her hand resting possessively on his arm. She was jealous, hating her rival and afraid of her power. "How can a thing like that bear children?"

"She can't," said Daroca. "She is trying to upset you, Mayenne. Don't let her do it."

"But if she could," mused Chom, "what children they would be. Gods and goddesses to gladden the hearts of all who saw them. My lady, I am a humble person and do not look as fine as I once did, but I would love you forever if you would make me the same offer."

Smiling, she said, "You are not necessary. Soon you will leave. You will all leave, aside from Earl and the woman. I can use her."

As a receptacle for the affinity-twin. Dumarest glanced at the Ghenka, cursing himself for the danger he had put her in, the trap he had been unable to avoid: Tormyle's mind in Mayenne's body, sensing her every emotion, experiencing what it was to be a real woman at last.

He said harshly, "You can't do it, Tormyle. It wouldn't work."

"It will, darling. I have assurance of that."

From whom? Chom? The entrepreneur was standing, puzzled, his face creased in a frown. Karn? He had eyes only for his ship. Daroca? He stood, bland, the hand bearing the ring stroking the side of his face. Himself? But if Tormyle could read his mind, why had it forced him to disclose his knowledge?

Had it been another whim? The desire to show him who was the master? A feminine willfulness induced by the shape it wore?

"No," he said. "I warn you, Tormyle. If you take over Mayenne's body I shall kill it. Do you understand?"

"More than you, I think, Earl," she said lightly. "You love Mayenne. I shall become Mayenne. When I do, you will love me. You will not kill the thing you love. You see, darling? It is all so beautifully simple."

The elementary logic of a child, but in the field of human relationships logic was of minor importance.

"I would kill her," he said flatly. "For her own sake, if nothing else. And you are wrong about me loving you. It wouldn't be like that. I would know that you were an intruder. If you've learned anything about love at all, you must realize that it is more than the desire for a body. There is a heart and mind and personality, a warmth and affinity which defies chemical analysis. She has it and you do not. As I told you before, you aren't a real woman. You are nothing more than a beautiful pretense."

She said coldly, "You could never love a pretense?"

"No."

"You fool!" Her voice was acid, devoid of all affection, the snap of a woman scorned. "Look! See your friends as they really are!"

It was an illusion, thought Dumarest; it could be nothing else. Karn was all metal and crystal, a hard, programmed mechanism with set paths and robotic ways. He gazed at the object of his worship, the world in which he lived and traveled between the stars. Chom was softness

and oozing slime, decay and naked greed, feral hunger
and a thousand grasping tentacles. The others?

He had the impression of webs, of spider-shapes
crouching, scarlet, shaven, robed and bearing a hated seal.
Then the moment had passed and all was as before.

Daroca lifted his hand and touched his cheek, his ring
spilling fire. "You know. I can tell it by your eyes."

"You and Mayenne," said Dumarest thickly. "Agents of
the Cyclan."

"There were agents on every ship in the area. Your
probable paths were extrapolated and snares set before
you. But you must admit that it was neatly done."

"Very neat," said Dumarest, looking at the girl.

"It was a trap which couldn't fail. I knew you would be
suspicious and on your guard, but against a dilletante and
a Ghenka?" Daroca shook his head. "Gorlyk was a fool
who tried to live like a machine; it was simple to slip a
drawing of the seal into his papers. I did not underesti-
mate you, Earl, but with me to feed you scraps of information about Earth, the Ghenka to beguile you and
Gorlyk to act as a decoy you didn't stand a chance. On
Selegal you would have been taken. We had radioed ahead
and men would have been waiting, a ship also to take you
to a place from which you could never have escaped. A
trap which couldn't fail," he repeated. "If it hadn't been
for the beast, the damage, the one thing impossible to anticipate."

Luck, thought Dumarest. The thing which had saved
him before, that and quick thinking and his own, natural
suspicions. It was the one factor impossible to include in
any calculated prediction, the unknown element which
defied even the power of the Cyclan.

How much longer could it last?

Mayenne stirred and said, "Earl, you must believe me.
It was a job at first; nothing more than that. Just something to be done for pay. But later, when we became
close, I would have told you, warned you. You must believe that."

"It doesn't matter."

"It does," she insisted. "Surely you understand. I fell in
love with you. Really in love. I was glad when the ship

broke down. It meant that I didn't have to betray you and that, at least, we could die together."

"The logic of a woman," said Daroca. "But, then, all women are fools." He glanced to where Tormyle stood, watching, waiting, a peculiar expression in the shining eyes.

"You made a deal with Tormyle," said Dumarest. "Told it about the affinity-twin."

"Yes."

"What about Chom and Karn? Do you intend to kill them?"

"There is no need." Daroca smiled, at ease, in command of the situation. "They have been in stasis since your eyes were opened to the reality of what we are, and have heard nothing of our conversation. The planetary intelligence has been most cooperative since I showed it how to solve the problem of gaining your affection. When I noticed its penchant to adopt a female form I guessed the way things would go. Predicted, rather; even though I am not a cyber I have some skill. You know, Earl, too often we tend to become overawed by sheer size. A brain the size of a world can become just as confused as that of a man. However, that isn't important. What really matters is that I now have the correct sequence of the fifteen units of the affinity-twin. An eidetic memory," he explained. "A glance at the buttons was enough. When I give it to the Cyclan I shall receive my reward. Money, but far more than that. A new, young body in which to enjoy life. A fresh existence."

The bribe no old man could refuse, no matron resist. The bait which would tempt all those holding power into the net of the Cyclan.

Daroca lifted his hand with the flowing ring. "Don't try anything foolish," he warned. "I am armed and will kill if necessary. Now, Tormyle, with your permission, I will leave."

"Wait," said Dumarest.

"Why, Earl?" Her voice had regained its softness. "We don't need them. And you told me that I should always keep a bargain."

"The ship repaired and returned to where it was found," said Daroca, "in return for the secret which will give you everything you could ever want. A fair, exchange, I think." To Mayenne he said, "I must bid you farewell, my dear. Our association has been most profitable. I wish you a happy future."

He smiled and lifted his hand as if to wave.

Dumarest moved. He stooped and lifted the knife from his boot, the blade poised to throw. He saw Daroca's sudden look of fear, the realization that he held knowledge which Dumarest didn't intend he should keep. He had declared himself an enemy and would pay the price.

The ring on his finger spat a thread of fire and something shrilled through the air.

Then the knife was turning, glittering, reaching out to send its point crashing through an eye and into the scheming brain beneath.

"Mayenne!"

She was not hurt. The wild shot had missed and she stood, one hand to her hair, her face pale but very determined. As he watched, her hand plucked a gem from the bronze tresses. Before he could stop her, she had slipped it into her mouth.

"Good-bye, Earl," she whispered. "It is better this way. But I loved you. I loved you so very much, my darling. So very much."

The Ghenka poison carried in a jewel. Quick, clean and painless. At least she had proved the last.

Gently he lowered her to the ground, to the soft grass beneath the scented trees.

He walked through a parkland of emerald softness touched with scented airs, low trees and shrubs heavy with fruit and flowers, vagrant globes drifting in a kaleidoscope of form and brilliance. The playground of a child, the heaven of an artist, a haven of tranquillity and peace.

The ship had gone and with it Karn and Chom, to find themselves in familiar space. The bodies of the dead had vanished and Dumarest was alone with the woman-shape at his side. On the grass her feet were soundless and, when he closed his eyes, she did not exist. There was no warmth of human presence. She was there like the flowers, the trees, and like her they were fabrications of the moment, devices which could own nothing from the past.

She said, "Earl, I do not understand. Why did the woman choose to cease her function?"

The terminology of a machine. Harshly he said, "The girl was human. She killed herself. She died. She did not cease her function."

"But why? It was not the action of a reasoning, sentient creature. To destroy the prime function is totally illogical."

"Humans are not logical, as you should know by now. Mayenne killed herself because she knew what you intended and refused to be dominated."

Perhaps too because she was ashamed, and did not want to meet the accusation in his eyes, the doubts she imagined would be there. She killed herself to save him from an impossible situation, making the only restitution she could.

Bleakly he kicked at a rolling ball of purple and scarlet and smelled the scent of roses as it burst beneath his heel. Three others sprang from where it had broken, darting aside, teasing, offering distraction.

He added, "And because she had pride."

"Pride?"

"Something, perhaps, you wouldn't understand. In every man and woman there is a point beyond which they refuse to go. It can vary in degree and nature, but always it is there—an invisible line at which they call a halt. To pass it would, in their own estimation, make them less than human." He paused and then said, "What do you intend to do with me?"

"You know that, Earl. You have no need to ask."

"I'm not a pet, Tormyle."

"Call me Mayenne. I will be Mayenne and you will love me."

"No," he said flatly. "Can't you realize that your experiment is over? You have learned what you wanted to know and now it is finished. Be logical, Tormyle. There is no one else here now and nothing you can use against me. The girl is dead and, dying, she gave me freedom."

"Call me Mayenne."

"I'll call you what you are. A soulless, heartless machine which has somehow become contaminated with the essence of your discovery. Can't you realize how insane this situation really is? You, a planetary intelligence, demanding affection from me, a human being? Have you no logic? No pride?"

For a long moment she remained silent and then said, "Pride?"

"I'm a man; would it be sane of me to demand love from an ant? I could feed it, play with it, tease it, hurt and kill it, but nothing I could ever do would ever enable it to give me what I demanded. Not even if I fashioned a part of myself into a similar likeness. And there is more. No experimenter should ever allow himself to become involved with his experiment. To do so invalidates his findings."

A floating star tapped him on the cheek, singing with cadences of muted harmony. He knocked it away and it dissolved with a shower of trilling notes. Toys, he thought bitterly; compensation for what he had lost. These were fragile things to titillate the senses and provide a moment of amusement.

She said, "You spoke of sanity, Earl, not pride. Who are you to question my motivations? How can you begin to understand the needs of what I am?"

A prisoner, alone, crying for the touch of life, the common bond of protoplasm. He could understand that: the thing which made men feed scorpions and spiders, talk to them even, consider them as friends, as welcome pets. But never as lovers.

Madness, he thought. It was an aberration which had become an obsession, a blindness which had narrowed the universe down to a single point, a determination which could destroy him at a whim.

He said, "You have chosen to appear as a woman, so let us consider you in those terms. Mayenne is dead, therefore you have no reason to be jealous. The rest? You whine, plead, beg. The cheapest harlot in the lowest house would have more pride. Didn't you learn from Mari how we regard a woman who pays for love?"

He saw the tenseness of her face, the sudden hardness of her eyes and knew that he was hurting her, shocking her. To one side a clump of trees flew into the air, falling with a crash, a shower of dirt and stones.

"Stop it, Earl."

He laughed, deliberately feeding her rage, edging his voice with sneering contempt.

"Does the truth hurt, Tormyle? I thought that was what you valued: the cold, naked truth. Perhaps you can't stand it any longer. You've been alone too long, grown too conceited. Or perhaps you've become insane. Is that it?"

A chasm gaped, ran to within inches of his feet and then closed with a snap.

She said, "I could destroy you, Earl, and unless you stop talking this way I will."

"You could kill me," he admitted. "But what would that prove? That you are stronger than I am? We already know that. That you are more clever? I think not. If you destroy me, you will only have proved one thing—that you have failed. It would mean that you have become a petulant, stupid, illogical entity unable to either appreciate or understand a simple problem in human relationships; that your experiment has taught you nothing and that all the people you destroyed died for no real purpose." He felt his anger rising, his voice growing harsh. "Mari and the brothers. Lolis and that poor fool Gorlyk. Mayenne!"

"You hate me," she said wonderingly. "You really hate me."

He looked down at his hands; they were clenched, the knuckles white. Thickly he said, "I hate you for what you've done. If you were real, I would have killed you long ago."

"As you did the man?"

"And for the same reason. He deserved to die. But I don't have to kill you, Tormyle. You are destroying yourself. You have become infected with emotion and it will ruin your mind. Once that is gone, what is left? An endless quest for what you can never have. A search for contentment you can never know. I feel almost sorry for you. Pity you."

"Pity?"

"A human emotion which you have not yet displayed. Charity, consideration, concern for the weak and helpless. One day, perhaps, you will need it."

She stood very still, very beautiful in her resemblance to Mayenne, the light from the sky turning her hair into burnished flame. Then she changed a little, an inward thing, a hardness, a clinical detachment.

"Pity," she said. "An incredible concept—that *you* could pity *me*."

He tensed, waiting.

"Pity," she said again. "Pity!"

Then she was gone and with her went the trees, the grass, the drifting toys. Dumarest staggered as the ground became uneven beneath his feet, stones and boulders and pitfalls to every side. Above, the sky grew dark, the shimmer vanishing even as he watched. Air roared as it gushed into space, lifting a cloud of debris of which he was a part.

He was thrown high into the emptiness of space where only death could be waiting.

There was a sun smoldering low on the horizon, dullness mottled with flaring patches and edged with a spiked corona. Dumarest stared at it for a long time from where he lay, conscious only of the throb at his temple, the rawness of his chest and lungs.

He remembered the gusting roar of air as it streamed into space. The debris, the rocks and stones carried upward on the blast, the splintering impact as something had crashed against his skull. Tormyle must have saved him, flicking him casually to where he lay as a man might flick an ant with the tip of a finger. Pity? Concern? Charity? Who could tell? No matter what the reason, the planetary intelligence had saved his life.

He sat upright, fighting a wave of nausea. The side of his head was crusted with dried blood. More blood stained his lips and chin, marring the neck and front of his blouse, coming from the capillaries which had burst as the pressure had fallen and he'd tried to breathe in the void.

Rising, he stared at where he had landed. On all sides stretched desert, a sea of fine golden sand. He had no way of telling if the sun were rising or setting. If the first, he would be caught beneath its heat to die of thirst and exhaustion; if the latter, he could easily freeze. Nowhere could he see any sign of habitation.

The perversity of a woman, he thought. Tormyle could have set him down in the heart of a city or on a world rich with water and growing things. At least he was alive and he should not complain.

Wetting a finger, he held it high. There was no breeze. One direction was as good as any, but only the right one would offer hope of life. Shrugging, he began to walk away from the sun.

An hour later he came to a road running like a thread of silver over the desert. Now his choice of direction narrowed to a single alternative. Left or right? As he hesitated, he heard a thin sound from the left. A bee-hum which slowly grew louder and resolved itself into a wheeled vehicle powered by a noisy engine. A man sat in the front. He wore rough clothing, a beard and a broad, floppy hat made of woven straw. He slowed, halting as he came level with Dumarest.

"You in trouble, mister?"

Dumarest nodded, finding it hard to talk. He gestured toward his mouth. "Water?"

"Sure." The man handed over a canteen, watching as Dumarest drank and rinsed his head and face. "Man, you look like hell! You lost?"

"You could say that."

"Want a lift?"

The seat was hard, a board covered only by a thin blanket, but Dumarest relaxed on it as if he sat on cushions. Leaning back, he examined the sky. It had grown darker, pricked with scant stars.

"Can't imagine how you got out here," said the driver. "There isn't a settlement for miles. If I hadn't come along, you could have died. It's a bad place to be at night. Anyway, I can take you to town."

"Is it a big place?"

"Fair. Not big enough for ships, of course; they land on the southern plain." He was curious. "What happened? You been dumped, maybe?"

"Yes," said Dumarest.

"Nice going." The man was bitter. "The bucks think it smart to take a man out, beat him up and leave him in the middle of nowhere. You been playing around where you shouldn't?"

"I upset someone," said Dumarest.

"A woman?"

More than a woman, but he could never explain. He sat back, feeling the ache, the strain of past activity, the reaction at his near-brush with final extinction. But there were compensations. He had escaped the Cyclan and not even its most skilled adepts could have predicted where Tormyle had placed him. The pattern had been broken. Now they had to search for one man in an entire galaxy, not an individual following probable paths.

"A woman, mister?" The driver was eager for conversation. "She had you dumped?"

Dumarest was cautious; the mores of this world were unknown to him. "Not exactly. I had an argument with someone. You get many ships landing here?"

"An argument, eh?" The driver sucked at his teeth. "Those damned bucks! Lording it over everyone they meet. You ought to be careful, mister. The next time you might not be so lucky."

"There won't be a next time," said Dumarest. "How about those ships? You get many?"

"A fair amount. You got money?"

"I can work. I'll get the money."

He would get the money and the passage on the ships which would take him where he wanted to go: to where Earth waited to be found.